Kingdom's End

Royal Sagas 4:

King James to Cromwell

Betty Younis

ISBN: 1548476854
ISBN-13: 978-1548476854

For Lillian

Chapter One

December 1620

A dark fury filled Roman.

"Get off my estate you bastard! Be grateful that I do not pull you from that beast and kill you now."

Villiers looked down at him and smiled.

"Sir. I am here to take the Ladies Henrietta and Elizabeth. I shall do so. They will go to the Tower. And this . . . estate, this land where witches have practiced their occult skills, it is hereby taken from you. As of now, it reverts to the crown, which, kind sir . . ." here he gave a mock bow from his saddle, ". . . shall do with it as it pleases, perhaps passing it to another, more deserving, baron."

The night was cold and hauntingly empty like an oboe's solitary note. The flames searing off their torches alone reproached the endless black of the midnight sky. Whipping and turning, they hurled the darkness back upon its heels as they roared out their fanged warning. Beneath the jagged silence of the inky sky beat the hooves of the mighty destriers, bred for war, bred for chaos. As they galloped along on the dark and lonely road, they shifted as one like some surreal school of fish. The picture thus presented, why, simplicity itself, pinned upon time like a child's cutout dolly, as they careened through a bottomless, stark and empty blackness, an unseen hand moving them across an unknown landscape down narrow paths and rutted roads. The moon and stars had disappeared, disapproving of the midnight tableau set out beneath them, their light shuttered against the wind and the wildness.

Elizabeth had long since stopped clinging to her abductor. His grip round her waist spoke the words she no longer needed to hear: he would sooner burn King James at the stake than let her fall. She was the prize; she was what they had come for. They had stolen her away with their might, claiming a grand and royal decree for their actions, but they lied. She knew well they did. Her cloak, only a white velvet throw with a white satin lining, was clotted with mud from their long ride along the deserted way. Beneath it she still wore the simple lace gown she had chosen for her wedding and she shuddered continuously from cold and fear. Only the ruby cross on its heavy gold chain about her neck, beating gently in time with the rhythm of the ride, reminded her that this was not real, that her family would come for her if only she could hold out, if only she could hold on.

Without warning, the lead horse reared and those behind slid and thudded to a halt. The road forked, and a moment passed before the lead rider determined his path. But his horse was tired and lathered and chose to slow its pace despite his master's insistence otherwise. Elizabeth's captor rode even with him.

"Why do you slow, man? Get on!"

"Aye, but she will not, m'lord. We will have to give them all a moment to catch their breath." He leaned forward patting the sweaty neck of his mount as he spoke.

"We will not - can you not understand the King's own English? I said ride!"

The lead man turned, and the two mounts became entangled as their riders' voices rose. Her abductor's arm loosened from her waist and he waved it in anger and promise at the leader. Others began to pull close joining in the vocal fray and the horses began to paw and snort, turning viciously this way now that, suddenly uncertain of their role. Elizabeth saw her chance. With every ounce of energy she had, she hurled herself from the saddle, using the horse's side as leverage to push against. No sooner had she hit the ground than she began running back towards the fork in the road they had only just passed. A wild roar arose from the men, but for once, the luck of the night ran with her. The animals interpreted their masters' screams and sudden jerky movement, the chaos, as battle, and they stood their ground like great trees amidst a forest, for close fighting was what they had been trained for. As the men swore, trying desperately to turn themselves towards her she ran on. She had no notion of where she was but she knew that valuable time could be saved if her family knew which road the posse had taken.

Elizabeth glanced back over her shoulder as she ran. The wind blew sharp, lifting her hair and streaming it behind her like gossamer gold. She must act quickly, for they would soon have her once again. A boulder shouldered the side of the narrow dirt road and she ripped off her cross as she came abreast of it. With barely a motion, she half-tossed, half-lay it on the massive back of the rock and kept running.

"Come and get me if you will!" she threw over her shoulder at her abductors. But a quiet smile lit her face as her captor scooped her up again, turned, and galloped once more into the deepening unknown.

*****

He twisted and turned to catch every lovely angle of himself. Twenty-eight, tall, and such fine calves! He set one leg forward towards the mirror, toe on point so that his new silk stockings took the light just so. It screamed parvenu, but he could not have cared less, for it screamed wealth and privilege even louder. With a practiced hand, he flipped his dark auburn hair over his shoulder and smiled at his image. His beard, rakishly trimmed to a decisive point just beyond his chin, accompanied a mustache splayed whimsically at its ends. A high lace collar, starched and held aloft by whale bone. Velvet pantaloons, a vest sewn with pearls. Ahhh, he could have collapsed on the nearby bed in complete and utter happiness had he not had work to do. Carelessly, he picked up two nearby strings of more of the luminous precious pearls given him only yesterday by the King and coiled them about his neck. Ah yes, he thought, the King, my patron.

My patron. The phrase stuck in George Villiers throat as he continued to survey the courtier he had become in the looking glass before him. He insisted on thinking of himself as self-made, a man who had risen from the ranks of the lesser nobility to become the King's own man. He had, so his narrative proceeded, turned a brilliant mind and a handsome mien to his own purposes, thereby raising himself and his line to heights they had never even considered. But the good fortunes of the Villiers only began with their favored son's position with the King.

King James adored him, it was true. Even now, sick, alcoholic and more ineffective than ever, James held to their relationship as a drowning man at sea might cling to his ship's broken timbers. But as George gazed at himself and stroked his beard, he knew that his real genius lay not in the carefully cultivated relationship he had with James, but in the friendship he had established with the kingdom's heir apparent, James' only remaining son, Charles. At the thought of the younger Stuart, George winced, aware that he was preening as a means of procrastination. Reluctantly, he moved to the small writing desk which occupied the central window nook of his quarters at Greenwich Palace. With a sigh, he took the chair.

Prince Charles had been adamant about the arrangement. He knew, he had explained to his friend Villiers, that only he could make it happen.

And so George Villiers began to write. On and on he scribbled, knowing that it mattered not what words he chose to put upon the page. No one would ever see them for what they were save himself.

Finally, In a wicked, smug way, he dipped the quill tip one last time, tapped it gently on the rim of the little ink jar, and made a grand flourish before putting his head down and carefully, neatly, penning an impressive forgery of King James' signature.

"There! Still have the touch, I say." He spoke only to himself, picked up the tortoise shell blotter and rolled its wool felt surface over his monarch's name.

Once again to the mirror. Dressed too grandly for the coming event, he decided, he called out for his man. Now, what would a beastly kidnapper wear? No, that was not the thread. He started over. What would a righteous soldier, the King's own man, wear on a midnight mission commanded by the sovereign himself? Villiers giggled and glanced at the command he had just written for himself to himself and by himself.

As his servant moved about, garbing him in what Villiers believed the occasion called for - dark leather and rough woolen garments, but all sewn with the half thistle, half rose of the crown - he called out again, this time with a message for his henchmen.

"Tell them I said haste! We must catch what light we can and seize the coven with surprise and stealth! Hurry now!"

Could they stick this work, he wondered? He jammed his sword in the belt which now girdled his waist, gave a sidelong glance to the looking glass - very nice indeed - and went to find out.

*****

The sun's rays slanted upon the horizon, signaling that the hour set for Ben and Elizabeth to be joined was upon them. Elizabeth twirled in her room before Anne, feeling the soft, luxurious fabric of the new chemise she wore beneath her gown. Weeks earlier Anne had appeared from the attic with a mysterious item wrapped securely in soft wool. Inside Elizabeth found the gown she now wore – a simple yet elegant wrap of cream velvet overcut with rose satin. It was beautiful, and her blue eyes glowed as she prepared for her nuptials.

As the bonfire blazed and the candles flickered in the twilight, Elizabeth walked the ancient aisle of Coudenoure's ruined chapel. The light illuminated her face like that of an angel before the divine. A stout baritone voice intoned a passage of holy gospel from the King James Bible. Flowers were strewn in her path, and each citizen of the estate stood in awed silence as she passed.

Light from a fire shone and flickered over the top of the high perimeter wall, casting a shadow even upon their own lit torches.

"This is it?" came a dark mutter from the back of the cadre. "This is the fabled Coudenoure?"

Is it? Villiers uncertainty was reflected on his own face. They had ridden hard and fast, but he was certain this was the place. But . . . surely

Charles did not expect him to risk all for such a slight and inconsequential estate! He checked himself, for he knew well that Coudenoure was not what drove Charles forward in frenzied lust. No indeed. Before others could voice their sentiments and doubts, he sent a scout to reconnoiter.

"There is the gate and mind you do not be seen. We wish to be certain of this place, and John," he paused here, ". . . find out from whence that great light comes. It appears to be a bonfire, but why would they build one on such a December night as this?" He pulled his cloak round him as though to emphasize his meaning.

As John Felton slid from his saddle and disappeared into the darkness, another man spoke from the shadowy rear of the troupe.

"You have not told us why Prince Charles wishes ill on this family, nor have you said why it is tied to the two women you have described to us."

"They are witches." George's reply fell heavy on the damp night.

"Witches!" exclaimed another man. "Surely you jest, man! We stand with you, Lord George, for you are our patron at court. But . . . witches! What folderol is this?"

George turned his huge steed to face them all squarely.

"'Tis not my idea. Our good King James believes it to be so, and therefore we aid him in his efforts to rid the kingdom of such evil crones."

A low murmur went round. They had all heard the tales of James' obsession with the dark arts, but like others, they believed he had left it behind when he came forth to rule England. The hesitation flowed like a sparking current through their midst. James spoke hurriedly.

"Why, you all know, surely, of how the King has berated his own priests and those across the land, demanding they preach warnings concerning the transgressions of women. Am I right?"

A dull and silent nod.

"Indeed. Sermons against the sins of women, sermons ordered by the King himself, and yet you doubt our sovereign's belief in their evil, seductive ways?"

A lone voice from the back finally spoke up.

"Sire, surely you do not believe in witches, nor does our King! He left that behind in that god-forsaken land up north."

George gave the man a crooked, knowing smile.

"Tell me, William, do you think a man writes a tome setting forth his beliefs in this matter or that, only to change his mind at a later time? Um? No, it is not the way of man."

He paused – he had not anticipated having to convince his own troops.

"How much more so, then, would a non-average man. Our sovereign wrote a very lengthy book – *Daemonologie* – on the subject . . . God's liver, we are here on the King's business! Quiet your fears."

John appeared panting heavily.

"Sire, it looks as though there is a wedding taking place in some chapel ruins."

"In December? Why the bonfire?"

"For light?" Came John's hesitant reply. "Warmth?"

"How many?"

"Bonfires?" A man in the back asked.

"No, you nit. People."

"Oh, sire, not more than fifteen or perhaps twenty," replied John.

"Weapons?"

"It appears to be a wedding . . ." John reiterated somewhat drily. "The bride is quite lovely."

"The bride is likely one of the coven - let us focus on her and her mother, for James told me that long ago, when he visited Coudenoure, the two of them did not even have the grace to be ashamed of their devilry."

He turned and dug his spurs into his mount while raising his sword theatrically, causing his horse to rear.

"We ride!" He screamed gallantly.

"WAIT!!" Came a chorus of voices.

Villiers snorted - he was robbed of his great moment.

"Where are we taking these women? To the Tower?"

Villiers shook his head.

"No, for it would become known. We shall take them to my estate and hold them there until the riffraff of their family disband and go away."

They galloped through the marble and limestone gateposts.

"You think they will simply go away?" John mused to himself. "Really?"

*****

They had been warned. As Villiers read the false decree demanding the surrender of the witches Henrietta and Elizabeth, Ben stepped forward to defend his new bride. Roman and Ian followed suite while Henrietta whispered frantically to her Aunt Anne.

"Anne, take Elizabeth and flee - you will be safe in the priest hole behind the mantel."

But Elizabeth refused and stared with burning anger at the men come to purloin her away.

"I stand with my family."

Evan as she spoke six men threw themselves from their saddles and began shoving their way towards her and Henrietta. In a flash, they had flanked Anne and Elizabeth. In a final desperate act, Anne turned to her niece.

"Run, Henrietta! Run!"

She then turned back toward their assailants but not in time to avoid the slashing wound delivered to her mid-section. A strong hand grabbed Henrietta's and pulled her from the fray. Farther and farther towards the manor house she and her unknown savior fled until a small light blinked forth from a door embedded in its heavy limestone walls.

Without a glance behind they ran through. The light was extinguished and the door pulled tight. Henrietta stopped, out of breath, terrified, enraged.

"Who are you, sir, and . . ."

The man turned. It was Marshall. Henrietta almost wept.

"Marshall! What is happening - we must return! Elizabeth and Ben are in trouble!"

Marshall shook his head, and looked with kindness on the woman whose family had saved him, saved Ben and saved Rouster from the streets of London. With Queen Elizabeth's help and love from Coudenoure, the three had slowly healed over the years from their early traumas and had pursued their passions: Rouster the chef at Coudenoure; Ben the scholar and librarian; Marshall the groomsman for Greenwich Palace. It was there, earlier in the day, that he had learned of Villiers plan and ridden to warn them but had managed to arrive only scant moments before Villiers' mob.

His gaze left Henrietta's distraught countenance and moved to that of Rouster. They nodded and moved Henrietta towards the library. While Rouster pushed firmly on a chosen spot beneath the lintel of the great mantel, Marshall pushed a plinth. A small opening appeared on the side.

"Henrietta, go. We will save Elizabeth but you will only be safe now if you are hidden. We will return for you."

Henrietta bent low and looked down the narrow flight of worn stone steps to the darkness below. She knew Rouster and Marshall were right and that they were fighting for her safety, perhaps even for her life. But she could not.

She stood and backed away and Marshall saw her resolve. In silence, he and Rouster closed the mantel, wondering what now would come.

"Quick, Marshall, Henrietta, hear what I have to tell." Rouster began speaking in short staccato clips.

As he spoke, his wife Mary appeared from the darkness, breathless and wide-eyed.

"Done," she whispered in a frightened voice.

"Check the chapel ruins for wounded, for we know not the outcome. What of the children?"

"The children and the others are all safe now, but I must hurry. There are some still at the chapel – Rouster . . ."

Her fear was palpable. Rouster kissed her.

"Run, dearest."

He too ran with his compatriots but in the opposite direction, towards the great wych elm front doors of the house. But even as they yanked them open they knew they were too late. A great thundering of hooves galloped madly past, and on the saddle with Villiers, held firmly in his grasp, was Elizabeth.

The nightmare had only just begun, however, for as the horsemen rode wildly off into the night a carriage, brightly bedecked with torches and gold trappings, turned onto the drive. Rouster grabbed Marshall's arm knowing full well what it portended.

Quickly they moved from the doorway to the side of the sweeping gravel frontage of the estate. Rouster was not mistaken. As the gilded cage drew near, a familiar face peered excitedly through the window. Six black horses, in the King's own livery, breathed mist into the cold night air. They arced round the outer perimeter of the pebbly way and pranced to a glittering halt before the enormous medieval doors of Coudenoure. Before they finished pawing and snorting a footman leapt from beside the driver. No more than a boy, he nevertheless exuded supreme confidence as he bowed to the face behind the glass and opened the carriage door. It was her.

Alexandra. The woman with enough charm and exotic beauty to hide the gall which lay beneath. Almost. But almost, apparently, had been enough for Prince Charles. It was said he fell under her spell when she was presented at court along with her father, the newly appointed ambassador from Malta. She had turned a blind eye and a deaf ear to King James' demonstrations of cruelty towards his heir at the ceremony, choosing instead to offer the gawky teen a shy smile of support. It was enough – he was smitten.

'Almost' had also proven adequate to ensure infatuation with the new woman at court on the part of the male courtiers of King James. They tripped over one another in their efforts to impress, to amuse. The King's rose gardens were bare, denuded by suitors in quest of the beautiful and mysterious Alexandra from the faraway courts of Malta. But Alexandra kept her flirtations with them to a minimum. She clearly had bigger game in mind, and teased the boys (as she called them in her silky Italian accent) only to increase her desirability in the eyes of her chosen target.

But 'almost' had not been sufficient to fool the women of the court. Female servants and ladies alike quickly tumbled to Alexandra. Should you be male, her voice radiated unequivocal warmth and erotic undertones even on the most banal of subjects. "Pass me a chicken leg" at the supper table had the same whispery rolling tones as an invitation to a midnight romp beneath the sheets. Should you be female, however, the request would be curt and demanding, if it came your way at all. She routinely ignored remarks and conversation by women and in a thoroughly fresh and novel way aligned herself with the men of the various palaces visited by James and his retinue. They could not get enough. The women, early on, had had enough.

As she stepped from the golden carriage provided her by Charles, Rouster and Marshall shuddered, remembering her previous visit to Coudenoure. With Charles in tow, she had demanded the estate, whispering in his ear about its proximity to Greenwich and the backdoor, almost secret path to its grounds across Greenwich Wood. She had batted her be-coaled eyes and sighed, reminding him how much more they could mean to one another if they only had privacy, if only they had an estate, if only she had an estate, if only Coudenoure belonged to her. In the blink of an eye, it seemed, and with George Villiers as an ally, she had accomplished her goal. She was now a propertied woman in her own right, one eligible to be queen. One day.

The doors gaped open, thrown against their hinges, squeaking as though against what they knew to be wrong. A further great creaking sounded as the footman hurried to the fore, bowed deeply, and opened them wider yet.

"Madame, welcome home," he intoned.

"Mademoiselle," she corrected him even while she breathed in the deep warm scents of Coudenoure. Ah, finally, she had a home.

"And see to it that our men clear these grounds quickly of all rabble according to the King's decree!"

Marshall and Rouster turned and quickly followed Henrietta, Roman and the others through the gates at the far end of the estate's drive. If Elizabeth were to be saved, time was of the essence. They had to accept the fact that further run-ins with the King's men must be avoided this night, even though it grated uncommonly rough to abandon Coudenoure without a fight.

Alexandra entered the manor house but immediately turned and called out for the carriage driver. The man turned, hesitantly.

"Wait. I have letters to return to the palace with you."

She called for writing materials and began a note to Charles. Her writing was slow and labored, as was her reading.

"My darling beloved Prince

"I am in our new home. Come to me.

Alexandra"

She signed her name with a flourish and immediately began writing a second note.

"Papa,

A sensual smile appeared round her lips as she dipped her quill and wrote on.

I am in my new home. Come to me.

Alexandra"

There! That would do – the words were simple but adequate to convey her meaning. She folded each, sealed it, and passed them to the groomsman.

"And see that each goes to the proper man, um?"

He bowed and left.

Chapter Two

The small party - Roman, Henrietta, Ben, Marshall, Ian - dressed in their finest for Elizabeth and Ben's wedding, huddled now in the dark brambles beside the gates of Coudenoure. Turned out of their own home. Too stunned to think, they clutched one another in fear until Roman finally spoke.

"We must save Elizabeth. She is blood - my child." The words were hot with emotion but frantic and clearly without a focused plan.

Rouster looked about at the sad spectacle and began gently herding the group forward. Ben had not spoken since his bride had been snatched from him at the altar; Ian grieved for Anne; Roman wanted action but could not collect himself. It would fall to Marshall and him to set them in motion in some organized, meaningful action.

"Come, come." Marshall spoke hurriedly. "Mary has seen that horses are waiting for us up yonder near the bend. Hurry, before we lose the trail."

They stumbled on until the soft snorting of the animals told them they had arrived. From nowhere a stable hand came forward with the mounts and lit torches with a small lantern.

"They will take her to the Tower," Marshall began. "We must stop them before they arrive for our chances become slim indeed once they've take her to the dungeon."

He noticed Henrietta preparing to mount. Her hair had long since escaped the old-fashioned cowl she had chosen for her daughter's wedding. Golden gray strands danced and streamed between the knots of its loose weave. Backlit by the torches, she was eerie, otherworldly. The maniacal determination written across her face only intensified the look.

"You must stay, Henrietta, for it will not be easy," Marshall said gently.

A strange and wild laugh escaped her lips as she threw herself upwards and into the saddle.

"You will not go with them, Marshall - you will come with me." Her words were cold steel. All looked to her with hope and despair for they had nothing else remaining.

"Roman, dearest, ride for Elizabeth with Rouster, Ben and Ian. Marshall, you will come with me." Her horse began to dance with impatience. Roman grabbed the reins, seeming to come alive as she spoke.

"Yes," he agreed, intuiting his wife's intent.

"What are you doing?" Rouster exclaimed. "We must go at once! What are you about?"

"Marshall shall take me to Greenwich, where King James is in residence. He wants witches, and by God and all the hosts of heaven I shall give him one that he shall not soon forget." Henrietta's words rang through the darkness like a call to arms upon a field of battle.

Too amazed to deny her, Marshall leapt into the saddle and they disappeared back towards Coudenoure, leaving the small knot in silent stillness. Finally Ian spoke.

"They took the life of my soul mate. Henrietta is right - we shall not allow them to take yours as well, Ben. Quickly to it."

Roman knew the old rutted wagon road well, and they raced on through the night following his lead.

*****

When the fires of the great hearths drew down and the candles cast dying, whimpering flickers of light against the dark shadows of James' palaces, when liquor began to speak its own loose language - it was then that the subject arose. It was not interesting nor relevant enough for daytime chatter amongst the ladies as they embroidered until their fingers were pricked red, nor was it gossip which seemed worthy of courtiers and noblemen. But deep in the night, when all other events, people, strategies and oddities had been carefully and wittily (or dully) dissected, ridiculed and tossed aside, talk at the courts of King James turned inevitably to past scandals of the court. Some were fabricated on the fly, grown and embellished even as the words rolled past some drunkard's lips. Some were true and some were half-truths, their origins buried in some long forgotten event or rationale. But of all the tales, rumors and insinuations, only one was ever discussed as a true enigma, only one stood outside the circle. Coudenoure.

The rumors of Coudenoure were vague but consistent. It was known that it was an estate - one whose lineage could be traced at least as far as the Field of Gold. This much had been confirmed several decades earlier by a curious and learned courtier. He had come across the name in Rutland's papers, and its recent usage had piqued his curiosity. Yes, it was there.

But the history of the place prior to that was rumored to extend even farther back in time. Henry VII, who visited the place several times while hunting, once wrote that it had the look of a monastic dwelling. The truth, as always, was much simpler and more deeply complex.

In Bosworth Field, since 1485, Plantagenet dead had slept a still and silent slumber with their archenemies the Tudors. This was no cemetery, but a place of carnage, a place in which Henry VII won the throne of England in hard-pressed battle. Henry had almost died that day, saved from a fatal wound by a simple knight, one whose family had no estate of which to speak. In gratitude to the man (one Thomas de Grey), Henry VII made him a baron and ceded him the small hunting lodge on the edge of his own great Greenwich Wood, the one he had visited - Coudenoure.

As for its monastic appearance and trappings, their origins were not clear nor were they researched. But whatever friary had settled there had long since moved on, leaving behind the estate which now came to the de Greys.

At first glance, as one turned off the brambled road onto the long, straight, gravel drive, one might note the isolated splendor of the place, the ancient chapel ruins, the great limestone blocks of the main house. The contrast of the pure and simple geometric lines of the place against the chaotic beauty of the meadow which abutted it was startling yet pleasing.

In the same manner, the family was said to be eccentric (some even referred to them as non-conformers), but also learned. They were isolated, but did not seem to grow inward as a result. The few who had known of them personally described them as gracious and charming.

That much had been established over the years of stewed words and random gossip.

But other, more interesting rumors swirled as well. Rumors about the estate's value to King Henry VIII, and to his heir Elizabeth. Talk of the wild red hair of the de Greys, so like that of King Henry, and of the artistic skills practiced even by women of the estate. Rumors of unimaginably beautiful tapestries and art. Why, it was claimed that there were even pieces by the great Michelangelo himself!

But the royal connection which made the rumors so delicious also fed a deep fear of royal wrath. That fear kept the rumors beneath the surface of court life. If the estate were indeed protected, special, even bewitched some murmured, it was best to stay clear of the place and its people.

Chapter Three

On the far side of Coudenoure, past the great ridge which separated its lands from Greenwich Woods, Henrietta pulled her horse up sharply.

As Marshall slowed beside her, they spoke in low voices.

"I have a plan," began Henrietta.

"Thank God, for I was beginning to fear your 'plan' was simply for the two of us to storm Greenwich Palace alone."

"That is part of it."

"Henrietta, Madame . . ."

"Just listen, Marshall, and you will see the wisdom of my approach."

Ten minutes later, they began a quiet and stealthy trek along the far side of the Great Ridge towards the back side of Coudenoure. They shivered in the cold as they approached the outer fields of the estate. Marshall had taken the lead and now held his hand up signaling a halt. They dismounted and tied their horses in a clump of nearby brush. Running lightly over the frozen ground they approached the row of craft cottages which formed a small alley behind the main house. On any given evening, the place was usually alight with house servants and craftsmen going about their daily lives. The miller could usually be found at the grindstone; the groomsmen in the stables; the yard boys about the business of loading tools in their wheeled carts before returning to the barns. Tonight, however, nary a light pierced the gloomy darkness. Even the stars seemed to shine less bright. Finally, they reached the same side door through which they had entered previously.

"Ready?" came a whisper from Marshall.

Henrietta nodded, and pushed against the door gently. She held her breath as the scraping of the door against its jamb lit up the silence like a living, breathing creature.

Pause and scrape. Pause and scrape. Slowly they shifted the ancient door until a wedge of light threw itself out into the night. Marshall went first, squeezing between the jamb and the door. After a moment, his hand appeared and Henrietta took it and stepped through. A long way down the central hallway a lone small candle glowed. All else was shadow and gray and still and silent. Henrietta wondered why the noise of the door had not brought someone running - she almost laughed aloud at the silliness of the notion when she remembered their circumstance. All had fled - Alexandra must be in the house alone. They waited, adrenaline feeding their senses.

She was right, for no one showed - their only company was the small candle far along the way. Henrietta looked up. It was seldom that she actually paused to notice the soaring spaces of her home. High above them the hallway arched upwards until gently curving in on itself, its ancient oak beams creating a perfect vault. The stones beneath their feet had never needed rushes or lavender to keep them fresh. They were swept and scrubbed daily. Down the way, deep carpets swallowed the echoes of the space.

Convinced they were safe, Marshall and Henrietta moved in stealth to a heavy door, original to the house. The room beyond had long gone by the name of Quinn's Workroom, named eponymously after Henrietta's grandfather. They slipped through quietly and Marshall pulled it closed behind them while Henrietta made her way haltingly to the fireplace. Feeling for a poker, she stirred the embers until an underlying level of molten heat revealed itself. Marshall used it to light a nearby candle while Henrietta looked frantically about.

What would a witch look like, she wondered. What would convince the King to revoke his own order and return Coudenoure to her family? Without warning her knees collapsed beneath her and she sank to the floor. Whatever wall had protected her from the evening's terrors had suddenly given way and she found herself shaking uncontrollably and near sobs. Her life, quiet as a breeze among willows, beautiful as purple bearded irises in the spring, sober as the calling of a sparrow carried on the light of dawn, all was gone. Elizabeth's twin, Thomas, had passed years ago, and she and Roman had now only Elizabeth. Anne had succumbed to the slashing wound inflicted upon her and now lay murdered on the ground of the chapel ruins. Roman, Ben and Ian were gone, chasing through the night. But should they find Elizabeth, then what? She had not allowed herself to consider the other side of Villiers' performance until now. Now, according to the decree from which he had read, Coudenoure was no longer the seat of the de Grey family. Instead, it was home to Alexandra. Clearly, if James and Villiers wanted a witch, they should look no farther than *that* woman. She put her head in her shaking hands and tried to think.

Perhaps her plan was flawed - if she went to Greenwich and appeared to James as a witch it might confirm him in his strange beliefs about her powers all right, but that might very well only lead to worse. Her powers, she snorted. She silently cursed herself for the day years earlier when James had arrived at Coudenoure and she had played into his superstitious beliefs about her. Her lie about a simple poultice given her by a simple woman to heal a wound had become a millstone about her neck. She was drowning, and taking her family with her. She sat stock-still and silent.

"Henrietta?" Marshall's whisper was urgent. "What is it?"

She had aged a thousand years that evening. Deep lines etched her cheeks and forehead. The cornflower blue of her eyes was almost gone, wrapped in layers of red and pink. Her face was stone white and still. Marshall wondered if she would make it through the night.

"What are we doing?"

The words shuddered from between her lips.

"King James might take my visit as an opportunity to imprison me, or use it to confirm his darkest ideas. I fear, Marshall, I fear."

Marshall sat beside her. Silence reigned between them for some long time. Finally, he spoke.

"Madame, you are correct. We must breathe deeply and think."

An almost hysterical giggle escaped Henrietta's lips.

"Think? *Think?* How would I do that with . . ."

Marshall interrupted with firmness.

"Henrietta! You must listen! Take a breath. Put all of those thoughts away for another time and focus on action, for I swear to you, if we do not act, and act wisely, then we will lose all. Do you understand?"

She sobbed and nodded, pulling herself together and stood.

"I believe my plan was based on anger and fear, and 'tis no way to meet a crisis, that."

Marshall nodded.

"And we cannot help those who have gone for Elizabeth - that outcome will not be determined by us."

They looked at one another.

"Henrietta, we must find a place for you to hide."

"Yes, I can use one of the workmen's cottages beyond the estate's rear yard. I am certain that Alexandra would eat cat dung with a filthy spoon before she would visit the homes of those beneath her."

Marshall smiled - Henrietta was coming back.

"And the workers – they will protect and hide me, I am certain."

Pause.

"And you?" she asked him quietly.

"I shall return to Greenwich. It would do us no good for me to be found missing on such a night. Once I am back, I will be able to ferret out what information is available and keep you apprised . . ."

"How will you do so?"

Marshall reached in his pocket and clinked several coins. Henrietta smiled.

"'Tis enough for now," Marshall met her smile, "But we will need more coin I am certain. Who knows what resistance Roman and the others are meeting. Should they send word to Coudenoure of such need, you must be ready."

"Aye. I have a chest but it is in the library priest hole. I shall bide my time and find a way to get at it."

They both breathed deeply, glad to be on stable ground once more.

"Let us go," whispered Henrietta. "When you reach the horses, give mine a thump and he will return of his own accord." She thought for a moment of the cottages, laying them out in her mind. "I shall take up residence in the farthest one, the one closest to the fields, across from the miller's wheel. Direct your messenger to that locale. Now come, let us go."

They retraced their steps. The light at the end of the great arched hallway still burned, showing them the way.

Chapter Four

Roman pulled up short and hesitant, forcing Ian and Ben to follow suite.

The road forked but he was uncertain which one lead to London. His mount was sweaty, and he dismounted, looping the reins over a nearby bush. He looked about but only the solitary torch still burned - all else was cloaked in blackness. The coal dark night, the circumstances, his heightened sense of danger - all contributed to an almost overwhelming fear that robbed him of any orientation he might normally have. He sat on a huge boulder and tried to think. He reached deep in his memory - *which way? which way?* - but nothing floated forward. He was lost.

It was the Matins hour. They had ridden steadily but slowly, finding here a huge hoof print, there a bush trodden down, and further on, evidence that yes, Villiers and his men had not turned onto some half-forgotten path but had continued on the road towards London. But now, this fork refused to give the troop of blackguards up, and neither Ben nor Ian could find a trace. Roman did not move, still trying to divine a course of which he could be confident.

The young boy who rode with them and carried the torch tied his horse and wandered down one fork, looking for any telltale sign of recent riders.

"What shall we do?" Ian asked quietly. He had had no time to consider Anne's death, her murder, and even now seemed focused intensely on finding Elizabeth. If anyone had noticed, his gaze and manner were too intense. It was as if he knew that a pause in their rescue effort might mean time to acknowledge what had happened that night and he fought against that moment with might and main. He paced to and fro before his companions.

Ben produced bread and cheese from a bag packed by Rouster's wife and demanded that they eat. He and Rouster both felt the oddness of his command: issuing a dictate to the two of them. They were his elders, and despite his deep learning and erudite approach to life, he had always deferred to them. In turn, to them, Ben and Rouster would always be the little urchins rescued by fate, Queen Elizabeth, and Coudenoure from a harsh and likely short life. And while, along with Marshall, the two had moved on from their days on the streets of London, that time nevertheless formed the underlying lens through which they viewed life. Those days also provided a mental toughness almost always missing in those who had never known such deprivation. Ben's bride was gone, snatched from the altar. Ian's wife was dead, and God only knew where Henrietta was. But of the four of them, only two were still thinking.

"Eat, we must hurry." Ben's tone was curt and authoritative. The older men did as they were told.

"We have no way of knowing which fork, but this one . . ." he pointed to the one on the right, ". . . this one seems to move in an orbit closer to the east. We shall take that one, and should we find no signs of their passage, then, after due consideration, we shall turn back and take the other."

Ben re-mounted and motioned for the others to do the same.

"Where is that boy?" his eyes sought out what was now but a small point of light as the lad with the torch had moved farther along the other fork, intent on seeking out clues left by the destriers and their riders.

"You there!" Ben called. "Come at once!"

The light seemed to pause in mid-air.

"Yes, come along now!" Ben shouted again.

Again the light held steady. Suddenly, it began to trace a jagged pattern up and down the sky. After a moment, it was discernibly smaller.

"What the devil?" asked Rouster but no sooner had he spoken than a childish scream split the frostbitten air.

The light grew larger illuminating the glowing face of the screaming running stumbling child. Yet he refused to stop or even slow his pace. The three men sat atop their mounts mystified. With a triumphant look, he ran toward them and held out his hand while bringing the torch close. Like an otherworldly light undulating beneath a watery surface, the rubies in the fabled cross of the de Greys held the torch's beam within their primordial depths, blinking, shimmering, as if sending forth a silent but unmistakable message. Without a word, the riders turned and urged their horses forward in response.

Chapter Five

George Villiers' estate was as grand as his creditors and his allowance from the crown would allow. Its official name - Heatherton - was oft ignored by locals, who preferred the name with which some unknown wit had dubbed it: Georgie-Porgie's Puddin' 'n Pie. Tucked deep within the rolling hills of County Leicestershire, it occupied the most prominent rise in the area. Sunrise and sunset were declared by the villages round about as the times when the sun's rays glinted steely and bright off the gold-leafed window frames of the place first thing in the morning and last thing at dusk. It was said that George liked to drag a chair onto his sweeping front lawn at those times in order to bask in the reflected glow.

The estate consisted of a jumbled main house, grown organically over the centuries by need rather than design. Its lack of organization, however, did not stand out against the further melee of squashed, ramshackle, hunched and squished outbuildings that dotted the surrounding landscape like scrub on an arid plain. An appreciation of random and loose intervals was essential to seeing the beauty that lay buried deep, very deep, within the picture thus presented. But what it lacked geometrically it more than compensated for through ornamentation. Turrets sat upon every rise of stonework like mushroom caps on a forest floor after rain. Like the window frames beneath them, they were gilded. Stone lattice work adorned otherwise beautiful ruins of aged lines and angles. The garden presented fields of grass that seemed to stretch clear through time and well into eternity.

George loved it all. Raised in a house which barely qualified as an estate with rather rigid lines and no bangles or sparkles of note, he felt Heatherton reflected his own risky rise: totally against the odds.

*****

The split maple marked journey's end, for the gates of Heatherton were barely two miles on from that point. The road widened some way back and was well-tended as though to announce to the traveler the approach of an important vista meant to be accompanied by awe and perhaps even inspiration. Sure enough, a final gentle curve deposited horse and rider on a deliberately widened mesa bereft of everything save empty space, and in the distance, something shiny and bright - Heatherton.

George had no interest in vistas, mesas, or inspiration on this particular evening. The ride from Coudenoure had taken longer than anticipated and, as a result, the dark ebony of night had now faded to a chalky gray. His arm was cramped from holding Elizabeth tightly on the saddle before him and Villiers was frankly grown weary of the entire escapade. At the moment when he and his men thundered through the gates of Heatherton, he could think of nothing else save freedom from the slavery of royal favor, from his dependency on it, and everything that went along with that particular fealty. He had done as his sovereign asked, but it lead to a personal question: how many more times would he have to participate in such tomfoolery? And not without risk. It was becoming too much.

They thundered to a halt at the steps of the manor house, and one of the men quickly jumped to clutch Elizabeth and pull her from the saddle. There was no need, however, for she was glassy-eyed with fatigue and apprehension, too tired to run again. With an easy motion he lifted her off Villiers' mount and looked up at his liege.

"Where to?"

Now there was the question. George had not thought this far along. The other men hung loosely in a knot about his horse. Someone from the back spoke quietly as though wishing not to be identified.

"Sir, she does not look witchish to me." His implication was clear - George was not the only one who had begun to have serious doubts about their evening's work.

"Witchish?" George shot back.

"Aye," came the reply, a bit louder and more robust than before. A shuffling of many feet.

"There is no such word." He threw his education and status in their faces, reminding them of his position.

"Why are we here, sir?" another man spoke. And this one stepped forward, challenging George. "Why did we not take her to the Tower where all state prisoners of the King are taken? If he himself issued the writ, why then have we brought her here?"

George had survived many challenges to his authority during his lightning-swift rise to power, and he knew well how to distinguish between harmless questioning with bite and actual threats. This had the smell of the latter. He had set in motion something dangerous and now struggled to get ahead of it lest it roll over him, crushing the life from his authority. He thought briefly of a flower press, each delicate petal arranged on the page before the turning of the screw brought down the weight which would freeze the tableau forever, its life oozing and seeping away into the soft paper. He jerked his mind back to the moment. These men were as tired as he was. Better to feed them and let them drink and sleep before the situation evolved further.

He smiled a winning smile, the one that always ensured the King's own favor.

"Let us not discuss the King's wishes until we have eaten and drunk our fill, eh? Once we have done so I will share the King's plan with you, you may be assured."

The idea of food and drink smashed aside like a sledgehammer any thoughts of revolt. George jumped from his saddle as though nothing had happened, nothing at all, and clapped two of the men on the back as he shouted for food and ale to be set forth in the dining hall. The crisis which had rippled outward from their midst passed on into the milky morn, seeking opportunity elsewhere.

"The girl!" someone shouted. "What of the girl?"

"Put her upstairs," George declared jovially. "I will deal with her later."

His companions did not notice the change in his smile, nor did they seek further information. George had not maintained his position in the

King's household - and heart - by being a fool. He was vain, he was crass, but he was not stupid. He had devoted only a mere fraction of his thoughts to the conversation with his men. The rest had been busy massaging the kernel of a plan.

King James, Villiers reminded himself, had no idea what was afoot in his kingdom the previous evening. Only he, George, knew of the treachery involved in the fake writ from the Palace; even his men were innocent of that knowledge. And there were two other small slivers of vital information which only he possessed. The first was that King James did indeed believe the women to be witches.

The King had visited Coudenoure and received from one of them a poultice which even now he wore about his neck. It had long since tattered away to pieces but James religiously had pouch after pouch sewn for it. When one pouch became too disintegrated for use, he would carefully place it, en toto, into a new one. He had been doing so for years, for he believed that no evil could come upon him as long as he wore the seal of the witch.

The second sliver also figured heavily into George's new scheme: namely, the women - Henrietta and her daughter - knew of James' belief about them. They knew of the book he had written on the occult, including a treatise on witches, and they knew of his thoughts concerning their 'powers'. When he had thundered in upon Elizabeth's wedding and read his false paper in a commanding voice, they had believed it to be true for the simple reason that they knew James' proclivity towards superstition and coven-craft - and of his conviction of their complicity in particular. There was no reason not to believe what their own eyes told them, and because their lives were threatened, they would continue to believe.

In short, these people had every reason to believe that King James himself had indeed suddenly turned against them and was now intent on preying upon them and their family. They would not go back to Coudenoure for fear of their lives and fear of the death usually accorded to such women. And in that false and deceitful evil lay George's salvation. Alexandra could continue to live at Coudenoure. He, George, could feel good about having pleased Prince Charles. And the poor rats of Coudenoure, well, not all stories have happy endings. As long as James was on the throne, Coudenoure would believe in the danger they had seen and felt that night.

The only loose end was the girl, Elizabeth, and if she were to escape, well, who was he to chase after her? After all, he had done as his sovereign heir wished. Besides, she was attractive enough - he giggled lewdly - surely she would manage to eke out an existence of sorts. And as long as she cleared his gates, his property, his *life*, why should he care? She knew not where she was and should she figure it out, she had no means to return to Coudenoure. No money, no means, a pretty girl. Yes, it would work out well for him. All that was left of this midnight folly was her necessary escape and he was confident it could be managed.

Life was fine, and he threw off his hat in the hallway of his great estate. As his men rushed for the dining room, George took a servant aside.

"Put the girl in the bedchamber at the rear of the house, the one on the first floor. And Joseph," he smiled charmingly at his servant, ". . . see to it that the fire is set so she might warm herself, and see that she receives food and drink." Pause. "And take care that the window be opened slightly, for I believe her receiving fresh air might be in all our best interests."

Joseph bowed, and George joined the others, happy in the thought that what might have proven calamitous was now merely inconvenient. A charmed life indeed.

So happy was he that he neglected to notice John, standing in the shadows, listening intently to his exchange with the servant. As Villiers moved away, John stepped forward stroking his chin.

Now why would George Villiers, Duke of Buckingham and the King's favorite, risk life and limb for a midnight ride, kidnap a maid, and then deliberately set in motion the circumstances for her escape? Hmm? He continued to stand in the hall, puzzling about the matter. The situation reeked of furtive motive and an utter lack of planning, regardless of the authority behind it. A young boy dressed in house livery silently untied John's heavy woolen cloak. He returned shortly and slid the long stout leather gauntlets from his hands and wrists, yet John remained still, in thought.

After a further moment, he turned and followed his comrades into the dining hall.

Chapter Six

"My *wedding* night. *Indeed!*" Elizabeth muttered to herself as the servant closed the door behind her. The fire in the hearth began to glow and as it grew brighter she moved closer to warm herself. A tap on the door and a small girl appeared carrying a tray almost as large as herself. Just as it might have tipped Elizabeth quickly took it from her. She curtsied sweetly.

"Thank you missus, lady, Madame . . ." her eyes shone large and round beneath her gathered cap.

Elizabeth smiled.

"Child, do not worry. Here, have some of this candied fruit."

The little one backed away, but Elizabeth's grin finally won her over.

"It will be our secret." The girl nodded and smacked her lips happily as she ate.

"Tell me, what estate is this?" Elizabeth tore ravenously into the meat and bread on the tray.

"Puddin' 'n Pie," the child spoke in a matter-of-fact tone. Elizabeth chuckled.

"I do not understand – is that really its name?"

"Oh aye," the girl helped herself to another fig and slid a slice of bread in her pocket. "Our Lord Villiers calls it Heatherton, but we all know it as t'other."

"I see." Elizabeth smiled and cut two large chunks of cheese, offering one to the girl. She wrapped it in another piece of bread and slid it, too, into her pocket.

"Ma'am, I must go, for I will be missed and was told not to speak to you and I do not desire a whupping."

She was gone even without Elizabeth's permission.

"Puddin' 'n Pie," Elizabeth mused as she continued to stuff food in her mouth. A small draft wafted past her and she went quickly to its source; the window was not only unlatched but even opened a crack. What? It did not take Elizabeth long to realize that she had deliberately been placed in a position to escape (there could be no other explanation), but she could not fathom the why of it all. Her hair, let down and luxuriously brushed full for her wedding was now beginning to irritate her. Rising from her chair, she yanked a sash from the heavy damask drapes of the bed and tied it back.

"Ah, better," she harrumphed to herself as she returned to the food. Her eyes were bloodshot with fatigue and her dress was tattered but she was refreshed by the heat and sustenance. She had no need to remind herself of who she was - a proud daughter of Coudenoure. Elizabeth was confident by nature, and by nurture. When it came to the education of its women, Coudenoure was asynchronous in many ways with its time, but no more so than in its treatment of the children of the crofters, tenants, workers and the De Gray line itself who were born and raised on its grounds. Education was considered de rigueur regardless of gender or station. Even the lowest and smallest amongst them received lessons in reading and basic mathematics. There were no children who were not fitted and trained for skilled labor as adults. The result was an odd sense of purpose that permeated the entire manor. Children grew with the knowledge that they, too, would one day find a niche with the skills thus provided. And for those whose bent might be more off the beaten track (perhaps they were attracted to the arts or scholarly pursuits), they were allowed to read at will in Coudenoure's great library; it was to this group that Elizabeth, Ben, and Thomas before his death had belonged.

For this cohort, their childhood had been spent unfolding and enacting the schemes proposed by Elizabeth. She had never doubted her abilities or compared them to those of others for the simple reason that they had never been questioned. She was a dreamer, but with the practical skills of a logistics master. And today, she needed every ounce of confidence Coudenoure had thus provided. She had heard the tales of Henrietta's imprisonment in the Tower as a young maiden. "If my mother could manage such a situation", she declared to herself as she continued to stuff food in her mouth and pockets, "then surely this problem before me shall not be allowed to spell doom for my own future."

Her thoughts now wended their way to Thomas, her twin who had died of plague. They had been so inseparably close, and even now she looked to him, spoke to him in moments of high anxiety or change. Despite the passage of time, she went yet to the small graveyard near the Chapel ruins of Coudenoure to talk to him, to lay sweet smelling spring blossoms upon his grave; lavender had always pleased him. She thought of him now, and imagined herself at his graveside, kneeling, asking for his spirit to be with her.

A chill such as she had never known passed over her.

"Thomas, help me," she prayed. "Stay with me, for I fear I shall falter without you."

Having tucked everything she could manage into her pockets, Elizabeth wished luck to herself, slipped over the sill and was gone.

Chapter Seven

Far away, a gray morning barely lifted the sky above the earth. All was mist as the scent of burnt oak and wood mixed with the other forest smells, its leaves and winter rot. In the chapel ruins the remains of the wedding had already frozen. The flowers from the glass houses, their petals turned to ice, dropped one by one in sad procession to the frosted ground as though mourning the previous evening's events. The fire, once glorious in its riotous tumbling flames, once dancing without inhibition across the altar space of the old church, was now spent. Nothing but dead embers remained. A mange-ridden dog was curled near the smoldering remains warming itself against the cold. The sullen breeze - the frosty breath of the icy sky - shifted course and brought with it the rhythmic sound of crunching metal. Repeatedly, the sound of metal against frozen earth and stone could be heard striking against the cold air. The dog's ears perked and it turned to trace the source without interest.

Barely discernible through the mist and cold was an upright figure some distance away in the graveyard of Coudenoure. Shrouded in fog and darkness, only upon close inspection did the one figure dissolve itself into a small group of men and women.

The women sat legs folded beneath them on the chilly ground, a shroud of cloth before them. They had thrown blankets across it as though to warm the dead woman within. The clinking sound continued as the two men who accompanied them dug methodically and quickly.

The grave was shallow as needs must be, for the ground was frozen and any minute the light might give them away. They were too stunned for tears.

One of the men motioned completion and they put their shovels aside. With the gentlest of notions, the shroud was lifted and placed in the grave. Flowers gathered in the face of deep fear but with determination were placed on its surface. Prayers were said to the Catholic God, for it had always been from that faith that Anne drew comfort.

No words were spoken as they mounded dirt over her. A single piece of limestone, pulled from a field nearby, was placed on top.

One of the women detached herself from the knot of mourners as they walked away, and moved to stand near the grave of young Thomas.

"Aye, young one, if ye hear anything, then hear your mother now I beg. Your sister is in danger. Help her, young son, I beg you."

A shudder as cold as the North Sea passed over her. Signing a cross, she moved quickly to catch up with the others.

Chapter Eight

Now what was that person doing out there on Heatherton's spacious lawn?

John watched from the dining hall window as the cloaked figure ran this way, now that. The silhouette was clearly staying in the shadows, but why? A sudden streak of early morning light illuminated her and he gasped - it was the woman they had risked everything for on behalf King James, the so-called witch. He stood chewing contentedly on a mutton leg as he watched Elizabeth zig and zag. She was proving more interesting than the talk behind him by Villiers and the others. He continued to watch while idly eating and considering the night's events.

So he had been right. Villiers had indeed set it up for the girl to escape - and of course, she was doing so, while he, John Felton, was a witness to the entire farcical scheme!

But what if he had misjudged? What if Villiers had unwittingly provided the opportunity for the maid's escape. Or perhaps he believed she would be too cowed by her captors and the night ride through the dark to make any such bold attempt. John had heard the rumors - George was pretty but not bright, cunning but not strategic - and perhaps this was a shining example of his deficiencies. He thought back to George's stated belief that the maid's family would simply accept the situation as a fait accompli. Even then he had questioned such nonsense. But what if he, John, were to catch the maid on her run? Eh? He reflexively began to stroke his chin as he thought. Why, perhaps he could improve his own fortunes with the Stuart line if were to capture her himself!

And what if he, John Felton himself, were to return her to King James rather than to George Villiers. Eh? John almost dropped the gnawed leg bone in giddy anticipation of the King's favors: gold, estates, perhaps a title for himself and his line! God's liver! He would have been successful where George had failed.

Trying not to appear excited, he threw the bone in the fire and wiped his hand on the linen towel thrown over his shoulder. Muttering about fatigue and ale, he ambled nonchalantly from the room and pulled the heavy door behind him. From the shadows stepped a small form: the same lad who had assisted him before.

"You, boy! Where are the stables? Take me to them now!"

The child pulled a candle from its wall socket, bowed, and led the way.

*****

Elizabeth stayed close to the manor house. Its choc-a-bloc nature provided seams of deep shadow through which she silently worked herself. Dawn had faded, replaced by the strange moody half-light of a December early morn. Silence, too, had stepped away leaving in its place the soft coos of turtledoves amongst the eaves and the stirrings of the magpies as they jostled for a sunny place in which to preen their shiny purple-black and white feathers. A raven, perched on the bare branch of an aged elm watched Elizabeth with curiosity, cocking its head now this way, now that, as it followed her shadowy run.

She could see the road beyond the wintry scene in front of her – the frozen brown of the lawn followed on by a bare copse of stately trees. Close, but not close enough. For a solid two hundred yards there was no cover. Should she break from the shadow, she would be completely exposed with no place to hide. She hesitated and considered her options.

Her mind returned to the room in which she had been sequestered. A ground floor chamber with a roaring fire and plenty of food and drink; a window left tantalizingly cracked; the rushed exit of the servant girl. It was intended that she escape, but why? Did they mean to scald her with her efforts by recapturing her?

She snorted to herself. The minds of simpletons had always annoyed her, and never more so than when their murky thoughts proved too illogical for her to follow.

"Just do it, girl," she said softly, "For ye have nothing to lose."

She set off at a dead run across the frozen turf. There was no point in pretending she was out for a stroll, nor was there purpose to be found in ducking or dodging. Her sodden cloak and gown streamed out behind her; the sash on her hair worked its way loose and fell to the ground.

"Make the trees. Just get to the copse."

On and on she flew, willing her feet faster and the road closer. A yard boy with shears and a barrow looked up from his own path nearby and watched her run. Had her breath not been ragged she would have breathed a sigh of relief for he seemed not interested in the wherefore of the spectacle before him; after a short moment, he returned his attention to his work.

With a shuddering gasp she crossed the shadow of a tender sapling. Another shadow fell upon her, then another. She had made the wood. But the exhilaration she felt was short-lived. If her family were to help, she must make the road - otherwise they would not know to enter the gates. She bent over to catch her breath and calm her nerves. Looking behind her towards the estate, she scanned the scene for signs of her captors riding once again to capture her. But the scene was quiet and peaceful and deserted, save for the child with the barrow. A lone hawk circled above.

Her run slowed to a trot and as she reached the road she turned to look for the crooked sapling she had consciously noted the night before - it lay to the left of the heavy gates and told her that salvation lay in that direction. Moving to the far wooded side of the road, she ran on.

Mile after mile slid beneath her tired feet. Between the estate and the split maple an effort had been made to straighten the road, to drown the rural nature of the place beneath straight lines and deliberate allees. Beyond that, however, it reverted to its original use: a market road for vendors and farmers, for crofters and tenants. Round a coming bend, she saw a long rise with a flattened area at its crest. There she would rest, she told herself, perhaps even close her eyes for a moment, for surely if they were coming for her they would have done so already.

She took the bend and began the arduous climb, slowing to a gasping walk at the top. Boulders laid down a rough circle around the crest but she doubted it was their natural state: Looking over her shoulder from one of them, she could see the gold of Heatherton gleaming in the distance. Elizabeth fished bread and cheese from her pocket and ate ravenously, licking up the crumbs when she was done. The food, the warmth from the sun, the emotional and physical fatigue suddenly hit her like a hammer's blow.

"Perhaps I shall rest for just one moment, here, behind this rock. If I curl tightly, should anyone pass they will not notice me at all."

She pulled her cloak close and lay behind the stone.

"Yes, this will do, but I shall only take a moment. That is all. I shall rest only one moment. One small mo . . ."

Her eyes closed before she could finish the sentence.

*****

The sun was well up and illuminated the flattened crest of the road. Roman pulled his horse in. Like its owner, it was too tired to do more than stop in its tracks. Behind him, Rouster, Ian and Ben did the same. They oozed like viscous liquid from their saddles, flowed to the nearest boulders to sit, feeling heavy and land-bound with the sudden cessation of galloping in their bones. No need to tether the mounts - they would go nowhere. In the distance, the golden spires of an estate glinted.

Roman found a large boulder on the side of the wide crest and lay back upon it, closing his eyes. Was it only this time, yesterday, that he had owned Coudenoure, owned its joyous celebration of his daughter's wedding, owned happiness? He lay exhausted by the world and closed his eyes to shut it out. But the move was pointless, for the gray shock of the past day permeated his being.

So tired were they all that no one spoke, each lying on his own boulder, each silent. Nearby a rustle of leaves, a sudden pip of an anguished call: a fox had caught his breakfast. A bird calling overhead. The absolute stillness of a cold rural day. A galloping of thunder rising over the ridge, coming closer.

Wait, what? Roman pulled himself from his fatigue and sat up. Yes, someone was coming. He gave a low whistle to the others and they pulled together and stood mid-crest. A black beast, almost twice the size of their mounts, appeared before them snorting and rearing. Still they stood their ground. The rider pushed back the heavy scarf which covered his face to reveal an unshaven, small-eyed and narrow-faced man with a gaping maw of rotted teeth. No one moved. No one spoke. Rouster noted the long sword which swung from the man's side; he noticed, too, the hand twitching upon it; between the four of them, they had only one short sword, and he was not sure any of them knew how to use it. Such was Coudenoure.

"Where is she, you bastard son of a whore? Where is my *wife*?" Ben spoke with a ferocious growl and stepped forward. Even his companions glanced nervously at him, for he was a quiet, scholarly man, not given to outbursts. The man in the saddle nudged his mount forward and grinned at Ben.

"So, ye wee lad, you married the witch, eh?" John did not believe the maid to be a witch, but needled Ben with the label anyway.

With no warning and no plan, Ben roared and threw himself halfway into the man's saddle, grabbing his clothes as hand holds and pulling himself up. A vicious kick to the horse set it trembling and stamping. Round and round the spectacle went, Ben clinging like a barnacle to John, tugging with all his might to dislodge him; John shouting in a tired, semi-drunk rage while slapping at Ben.

"Get off me you rat's dung!!" shrieked John.

"Dung is a collective word, you ignorant worm!" Even in the midst of a fight for his life, Ben could not tolerate poor grammar. "Now where is she?"

But even as Roman, Ian and Rouster began to circle the theater before them, John reached for his sword.

"Enough!" came his cry.

But no one paid attention or even heard his throaty cry. Something half-human, half-animal, beige of color and furry in appearance with a gnarled and knotted mane streaked from the edge of the crest. The scream it loosed upon the woodland melee curdled milk for miles. The monster was beside Ben in a split second, sinking its teeth into John's sword arm and grabbing the blade from him.

"Heeeeaaaawwwwhhhh!" It threw itself away from the horse and sliced at John's leg. Ben let go in startled fear and John tumbled off. John rolled to defend himself from the demon.

"AAAAwwww! DIE YOU BASTARD!" Another slice to John's mid-section.

In a matter of mere seconds, the beast had come, been upon him, and knocked him to the ground. At the very moment it began spewing words, they recognized it as their own.

"Daughter!"

"Wife!"

"Niece!"

Elizabeth stood more glorious than at her wedding - proud, straight, hissing and feral.

John scooted back across the ground turning to crawl and then rising on his knees to run. As he made for the far side of the crest, Elizabeth ran after him with great slicing arcs of the sword.

"See that ye tell your master what the witch of Coudenoure has done to you. AYE!! She will do the same to him should he ever approach her again. Brews and potions for both of you and all your family. Now run, weasel, run! A pox be upon you!!"

She halted and watched as he held his mid-section and limped-ran out of sight. The sound of his footsteps fell away, leaving a deafening silence in their wake. A lone rook on the rise settled back amongst the trees with no sound, songbirds ceased their calls. No rustling of leaves interrupted the roaring break of earth noise and human speech. Elizabeth turned.

Roman, Ian, Rouster and Ben stared at her in pale and obedient silence. If she had stepped forward, there was a chance they would have run, or at least recoiled in self-defense. A tired grin split her filthy face and she brushed her matted hair back with an equally dirty hand.

"Now aye, that is how a witch - and a woman - defends herself," she laughed. "T'will be a cold day in the devil's own hell before they come for me again!" She looked down and picked a twig from her soggy dress, then looked at them again with an innocently wicked smile. "Do not you agree?"

Ian let out a howling laugh. Ben ran to her. Roman collapsed on the ground.

They were on their horses in an instant, Elizabeth securely tucked behind Ben.

"Ride on!" Roman shouted.

Rouster laughed aloud despite his deep anxiety.

"By the by, dear," Elizabeth half-shouted half-whispered in her new husband's ear, "Dung is not a collective. It may on occasion be used in a singular application."

She could not see the smile on Ben's face, the first since her kidnapping.

"I say, my husband, do you not hear?"

He laughed jubilantly.

"Today, my love, you may say and do anything you wish, for what was lost is now found."

She nestled her head on his shoulder.

"Even if," he added tartly with a grin, "you are mistaken."

*****

John limped like a wounded dog through the gates of Heatherton. His abdominal slice was not deep but ached with the season's cold. But that was not his concern. His leg still oozed from the deep cut the witch had inflicted on his thigh. And his horse! Where was the beast? Eh? His thoughts turned dark and cold with revenge but he could not bring himself to utter a single word about the morning's events, much less his antagonists. Whether a newfound belief in witches and their power, or wounded pride motivated his silence he did not know, for John was not a deep thinker.

That woman had taken him down, turned him flailing from her blows and fleeing from her fierce powers. And the men had done nothing. He recalled their faces and knew he had seen them previously, in the crowd in the chapel ruins. The one who had stepped forward, yes, it was he who had stood with the maid at the altar. He saw them also as they stood that morning on the crest of the hill - too stunned (likely too frightened!) to move. So this was Coudenoure? A place where women did not understand the natural order ordained by God on high? A place where men obviously lived in fear of their wives? He shook his head.

The copse flowed into the great lawn and he reluctantly began tracing his way over the icy turf, keeping his head low so as not to be recognized should someone espy him from a window. He had no desire to be seen, for what would his tale be - defeat at the hands of a woman, the very maid they had abducted?

He circled the manor house and made for the stables. He would get a horse, he did not care whose, and leave before word got out and questions came.

A boy sat idly warming his hands over a small pit of fire and Felton barked a command to him, following him into a nearby mews and down the way to the stables. He leaned against its brick wall, closing his eyes, waiting for the saddled horse to be brought forward.

"Oh, now, you are about quite early, are you not?"

John jumped and peered into a dark corner. George Villiers leaned against a large barrel, eating an apple.

"I am. I am going for a morning ride to view your lovely estate."

"Is that so?" Villiers stepped from the shadows. "Tell me, did some whore from the tenants' quarters do you wrong last night?" He pointed at John's mid-section then his leg. Finally, looking him up and down with a disdainful sniff, he threw the apple core to a nearby mare.

John said nothing. Villiers stepped closer.

"Be careful, John, for should I find that you ever went around me, ever tried to gain the King's favor over me, well, sir, t'would not be a healthy thing for you."

"Sir . . ." John began but Villiers had already turned and strode away.

"Bastard." He stroked his chin furiously.

The boy brought a horse and he was away, cursing to no one but himself.

Chapter Nine

Not far from the gates of Coudenoure a small child sat . . . and waited. Wrapped against the cold he noshed on dried figs and bread. It was quite exciting to be trusted to help Papa be part of the rebellion of last night. He kept a wide-eyed vigilance even as he imagined the outcome of the events. Fighting? Mayhem? He could hardly wait.

He felt the beat of the hooves before he heard them. The soft winter ground soaked up the pounding and sent it out through the fibrous winter detritus of a damp December. The child rose and moved cautiously to the roadside while a band of riders took a nearby curve in the old wagon road. They came closer and he smiled as he stepped into the road itself. The lead horse sagged to a stop, its breathing as labored as dry heaves. He ran towards it.

Rouster scooped him up onto the saddle in front of him while the others circled about.

"Well done, John. Now, tell us what you know."

"Mama says do not travel down the drive of Coudenoure, Papa. She says it will not do."

"What else?"

"She says you must go beyond the gates, even beyond the ridge, and circle round through the meadow to the fields beyond."

"Aye, that makes sense," said Roman tiredly. "Tell me young one, how many men are at the estate? Are they armed?"

John thought.

"Well, sir, there is the miller, and old sir Goland still runs the stables . . ."

Roman and Rouster laughed.

"No, no. I mean to say, how many enemies of Coudenoure are there? How many men that you do not know?"

"Aye, I see. There are none, sire. All have left. Mama says 'tis very strange, for there is a woman in the house but she is alone. Very early this morning, she sent the men who were with her off with a letter of sorts. I am certain we can win in battle."

Ian smiled at his excitement and spoke to the others.

"We must do as Mary says, for we know not what awaits us."

"And she says further . . ." John happily put another fig in his mouth, ". . . that you are not to ride your horses onto the grounds but leave them behind – she has posted a stable boy to care for them."

Ian nodded.

"You are to go to the empty cottage at the end of the row, near the shearing pen."

"Very well," said Ben. "We are almost home men. Let us hurry now."

Roman dared not ask the questions. Where was Henrietta? Did she yet live? And Anne? Was she still cold and alone on the chapel stones? He shuddered and braced himself for what they might find.

*****

Fatigue was no good to her. It made her fretful, felt rough against her being like stone polished against sand. Henrietta felt caged in by circumstance and her own foolish actions from long ago. She had slipped into the deep past now, weeping before the fire as she lashed herself with stinging remembrances. She could see herself with King James as clear as day, placing a poultice about his neck, not denying his belief that she was a witch, sending him forward in fear of her powers. What had she wrought!

She sat on a milking stool and mindlessly stoked the fire. The night had wrung the rage from her bones, leaving nothing but hollow fear and regret in its wake.

"This is all my fault, my doing." Over and over again she castigated herself with the words.

In the early morning, Mary had come to her, bringing broth and encouragement but no news. She had made the old bed which stood in the corner farthest from the door, had put covers on it and encouraged Henrietta to sleep for a bit.

"Where are they?" Henrietta cried out to her. Suddenly she rose looking wildly about for her cloak. "We must see to Anne's body, for I will not have her left alone there in the chapel. Help me, Mary . . ."

Mary forced her back onto the stool.

"Oh aye, Ma'am indeed, t'would be a sin before God were she left there. You need not worry, for we have seen to her burial, Ma'am, and she is safe in heaven now, away from the cold and evil that struck her down."

As she spoke, a rattle at the door came. Mary grabbed the sword she had brought with her while Henrietta pulled a small log from the fire - charred and blistered, molten heat. They stood together.

"Mama! I found them Mama! Look, Papa is here!"

Henrietta almost forgot to toss the log back onto the fire before throwing herself into Roman's arms. In future times, as the story was told, as it waxed and waned with each telling, she could never remember what happened after that. But it did not matter, she always assured her rapt listeners, it mattered not at all, for they were home and safe and sound.

Chapter Ten

Marshall rode like he was being chased by the devil himself. Deep soaring leaps and gallops across the field, tentative missteps and stumbles through the darkened wood of Greenwich. On and on - had he not made the trip a thousand times before he would have gotten lost. Cursing, snorts, farther on farther on.

The land beneath shifted for a final rise towards the road that fronted Greenwich Palace. Marshall flew on crossing it with two stretched leaps by his horse.

"Halt!"

"Oh aye, 'tis me, Jeffrey - Marshall. Raise the gate old son."

Marshall reined in as Jeffrey moved closer.

"Do you have some woman now? 'Tis about time! Is that where you have been?"

"Me?" Marshall replied with a grin. "If wishing made it so! And what makes you think I would leave the lovely lass - for she would surely be lovely - and come back here before dawn? Um?" He laughed. "*Indeed!*"

Jeffrey patted the sweaty horse's neck and motioned Marshall to lean close.

"There is some mischief afoot tonight, friend, and 'tis not good."

Marshall looked him in the eye.

"What kind of mischief? Is the King in danger?"

Jeffrey shook his head.

"'Tis not clear but I do not believe so."

"What do you know?"

Jeffrey lowered his voice to a mere whisper on the wind.

"You will not believe my words, but Villiers, the grand Duke of Buckingham himself, formed a band of trouble mongers and went in search of witches."

Marshall hoped his laugh did not sound forced.

"What silliness is that?"

"Aye," Jeffrey nodded in agreement. "I will know later, but it seems there is an estate nearby, Courderner-something or other or some word like that, and Prince Charles wishes it for his whore."

"Hmm," Marshall's voice was thick with encouragement for him to continue.

"I believe whether he should succeed or not, 'tis a bad moon over the event, and mark my word, it will haunt him."

Marshall straitened his back.

"We will keep each other posted," he nodded.

"Aye, and see that you do not go near the palace proper but circle to the far stable by staying amongst the trees. You should be safe that way. Get in your bed as soon as possible. And Marshall, you retired early, and slept all night - do ye understand me?"

There was no need for a reply.

Marshall fell into his bunk thinking not of the evening's strange and awful events, but of Jeffrey's words. It had come to him more than once that even as his friends married and settled into very domestic routines he had never found a woman of his own. His world was horses and stables, men and saddles and brass and hay and polish. While many had noted his leadership skills, he *himself* had noted his utter and ongoing awkwardness when faced with potential mates. Young women caused him to stutter and blush – and those times were the *best* of the lot. It mattered not who they were, nor what their appearance was. Sweet, beautiful, angelic and proper brought on serious nausea; short, ugly, noble and sly gave him severe cramps; anything in between was as painful as having a tooth pulled. His inarticulate and in his mind unexplainable behavior led to a general avoidance of women which led, in turn, to his present situation. He pulled the covers up and fell into a heavy sleep, dreaming of himself dancing at a ball with dozens of eligible women, chatting with them wittily as he swirled them across the floor. But even in his dream he knew it was nonsense, and that when he woke he would be lonely self once again.

Chapter Eleven

From the mist rolling in off the Thames a figure emerged on the long straight drive of Coudenoure. His saddle was deep walnut (likely new with its glistening oiled leather), his steed palomino. Its white tail and mane caught the rising sun and contrasted sharply against its golden coat. A more beautiful horse did not exist and like a kitten at play it danced sideways occasionally as it moved forward, wanting all to take note of its remarkable looks.

Even from a distance it could be seen that its rider was an older man - in good physical condition, yes, but with the onset of a paunch which strained against the elaborate brocaded buttons of his vest. As he neared, the silver gray streaks in his hair became evident, as did a much receded hairline. In the fashion of the day, he wore it long and curled, but the damp mist and its thin strands conspired against his best efforts, and it resembled nothing so much as a used mop as he rode gallantly at a stately pace up the drive.

Yet he carried himself well. This particular morning there was a youthful spring in his step and he practically bounced out of the saddle to the great wych elm doors of Coudenoure. An ancient bell was mounted on the limestone jamb and he rang it vigorously. No answer. Again he jangled it loudly.

Slowly, the door opened and rush of warm air escaped into the cold morning. No one appeared. After a moment, a feminine hand slid around it and beckoned him inward. A grin split his creased and weathered face and as he grabbed the hand a shriek of laughter and delight filled the hall.

"Oh, Papa, it is you!" Alexandra feigned surprise. She pulled her hand away, smiled, bent slightly forward and began backing away. Her silk gown was the color of the sky on a clear summer's day, and was sewn to accent her curves. Her smile promised more than morning tea and biscuits and Papa reached out to grab her. But he caught only air, for she skipped lightly backwards, still smiling. Again and again he tried: again and again she moved closer to the grand stairs leading to the bedchambers on the second floor. Finally he lunged, but she was quicker. Up she ran screaming with laughter and up he chased grabbing at the hems of her gown and chemise. They disappeared down the long hallway of the upstairs. Some moments later, a loud shriek of laughter was followed by a door slamming shut. All was silent once again.

*****

Mary responded tentatively to the mid-afternoon call from the library. Bowing deeply, she advanced slowly towards the man and woman standing before the hearth. Rouster had told her of this creature, had warned her, but Mary still gasped as Alexandra turned to face her.

"Why do you appear surprised?" Alexandra's voice was haughty, imperial. If the servants thought she would offer an explanation for the change in masters they were mistaken. Best they learn that from the beginning.

"Mademoiselle, it is because of your great beauty - I have never seen anyone so lovely, nay, never."

The simple honesty of Mary's reply caught Alexandra off guard - women almost never acknowledged her gift from heaven, her passport out of a difficult childhood, an impossible youth. She smiled in spite of herself.

"Where are the others?"

Before she had left the cottage, they had worked out an interim plan - all save her were too tired to move. Sleep was necessary and it was incumbent upon her to cover until Marshall returned, the others awoke, and all collected themselves. In the shepherd's hut out beyond the allee of cottages, the others waited: the stable hands, the cooks, the maids. All had heard of the family's return, all threw in their lot with the de Greys.

Mary turned her thoughts to the woman now before her with a practiced explanation.

"My lady, they were frightened by the events of last night, they were." Again a deep bow - obsequiousness was always pleasing to usurpers, "When they see that you are now mistress of Coudenoure and that you mean no harm to them, they will return, aye, for this is their home."

Buying time was the central plank of the strategy Mary now executed.

Alexandra considered this bit of information. It was novel to her that she now had employees, she now owned a working estate, she was mistress of her own stone and field and slate and stables' world. She rolled this round in her mind over and under. John Parisot, her companion and erstwhile father, looked sharply at Mary, so much so that she felt a jolt through her soul.

"What is your name?" he asked.

"Mary, sire, I am a housemaid and until the others return I will see to the mistress' needs."

"The mistress' needs and the *master's* as well."

He drew himself up and looked to Mary for confirmation. Yet another bow.

"The *master* and mistress will now have tea," he declared broadly, "Bring it with food, for I am famished."

Mary scraped her way backwards through the door.

"So what is this?" Alexandra had noted the sharp emphasis on 'master'. "Remember, *Papa,* that this is *mine,* was given to *me.* Is it not lovely? Surely you are happy for me?" She attempted to soften her warning with a pretty ending of pretty words.

"Alexandra, do not forget yourself, daughter. What is yours is surely mine."

He failed to note the hardening of Alexandra's eyes.

"No," she thought, ". . . for once, something is mine, and the fiends of hell will have me sure before I share it."

She smiled and nodded. Coudenoure may have come to her because of her beauty but she would keep it because of her wits.

"And after tea, we shall look about the place and see what we have, um?" she smiled sweetly.

Happy that she was back in her place and understood that he was now and would continue to be her master, 'Papa' moved to the table at the great front window to await his meal.

*****

Late afternoon saw yet another lone rider on the long drive. His mount, its livery, his manner - all reeked of royal privilege. It did not hurt that impression that a cluster of pike-bearing and helmeted guardsmen watched his progress from the gates. Mary recounted the happening late that evening to the other servants.

"Why, it was Prince Charles himself!" she said between mouthfuls of mutton stew. "And was not he dressed dandy! His stockings, oh aye, they were of such silk as I have never seen. His pantaloons were short I say, but 'tis the fashion these days."

All considered these remarks.

"It could not have been his own hair. It was as full as a maid's and curled to perfection. I have never seen anything like it!"

"And then what?" asked a stable hand.

"Well, he rode on and when he reached the doors the Lady Alexandra and her 'Papa' were waiting for him."

A giggle went round the room, for Mary had told them previously of the noises emanating from the second floor bedchamber that afternoon.

All leaned in.

"And would you know it, the Prince just sat upon his horse - a great black beast of an animal - he refused to dismount."

"What happened?"

"Papa was forced to get the steps from the side of the door and place them for the Prince's dismount!"

Peals of laughter.

"Pride goeth before a fall, aye, it is the truth." All agreed.

"What next, Mary? What next?"

"Why, you will not believe it, but the Prince dismissed him from the estate then and there! His beautiful horse was where he had left it - tethered to the post. Papa had no choice but to leave!"

Under other circumstances this disclosure would have been met with more laughter. But not a soul present failed to what was coming. Several sly glances and grins crossed the room like a silent wave of puerile emotion.

"Where were you, Mary? You watched all of this?"

"Aye." She spoke emphatically through a mouthful of biscuit.

"Then," she continued, "Prince Charles and the Lady Alexandra went inside. They seemed not to notice me! Of course," she giggled, ". . . I may have stepped into the shadows."

A nervous titter.

"And then the Lady Alexandra says, she says, 'Why *Charles*, did you know that Papa believes your gift of Coudenoure was to him! Not me! What say ye, my love?' And she actually put her hand upon the Prince's chest! Aye!!"

Heavy breathing and stunned silence.

"And the Prince says, 'Oh, no, my Alexandra – do not worry on that count, for Coudenoure is yours and yours alone."

Knowing she had them, Mary took another bite of stew and enjoyed it thoroughly before speaking again.

"And Alexandra slides her hand along his shoulder and says in a very strange voice, 'Charles, you have given me endless pleasure with this gift of yours. Come, I will give you the same."

Gasps. Silence.

"And for the second time today, my friends, she led a man up the stairs of Coudenoure, but this time," Mary cackled at the joke she had planned, ". . . this time she chose a *different* bedchamber."

It was the most titillating gossip any of them had ever heard; it would still be alive generations later.

Much later, as the moon waned and Charles slept, Alexandra lay awake. It was not that the Prince was now her man that occupied her thoughts, nor did they wander to the perfidious and dangerous subterfuge she was undertaking with a royal lover. This gave her no pause for the simple reason that she was a master manipulator of men's emotions. They were children, really. When forced to choose between nature and virtue, she had no doubts as to their choice. No, there would be no trouble from that quarter.

Strangely to her, she could not stop thinking of her mother. She lay, her arm above her head, twirling a lock of hair as she traveled back home in her thoughts. Malta, with its strange governance and Hospitallers, its sun-bleached beaches, its cobbled ways, its wharves and ships and sailors. She turned her thoughts away from the sailors, a dirty tribe in her mind. Her mother forced to use them for survival even as they used her.

But she had protected Alexandra with a fierce love, had recognized that she was gifted with a rare beauty. She had seen to it that she passed into other worlds, for her beauty was beyond compare and certainly beyond Malta's tiny reach. The fates decreed that in her, feminine beauty would reach fruition and that she, Alexandra, would sail away and leave her sordid past behind. Her mother had done what she had to do - and Alexandra had got clean away because of her efforts. As she drifted off to sleep she thought of her again, forever trapped.

That night, for the first time in her life, she slept in a home of her own, and some part of her was grateful beyond measure to the woman who had helped her escape.

*****

Charles left at dawn. He did not notice the lone figure in the graveyard near the chapel ruins. He did not see the man lay a blanket on the ground before laying down himself, nor did he see the figure place two heavy, warm woolen quilts over himself and the fresh grave beside which he lay.

He did not hear the heavy choking sobs which then filled the cold and empty air.

Chapter Twelve

It was late the following day before Marshall could fly back to Coudenoure. A child had been dispatched in the wee hours of the morn to tell him of the safe return of Ian and Ben, of Roman and Elizabeth and Rouster. He had spent the day collecting from the palace what intelligence he could.

He came up the back way and left his horse far out in the bushland bordering the meadow. In the distance, he saw two figures wrapped tightly together sitting on the old stone fence. It was Elizabeth and Ben, and he smiled, thinking of the tales they would tell their children of their first night as husband and wife. So intent were they in conversation they did not notice Marshall pass in the near distance and he left them on their own. Despite the long rays of the sun upon the horizon the place was abuzz with activity. Smoke rose from the chimneys along the cottage allee, and all but one of the great stacks of the manor house proper belched a black and sooty residue.

As he entered the allee, he saw Rouster coming back from the kitchen, Mary headed into the house. Goland was barking at the stable boys while the ancient miller drove his equally ancient oxen along the path to the feed trough. Two young kitchen maids were just leaving the glass house with a basket of fresh lettuce and broccoli; yet another appeared through the back door with a sack of laundry. It was busy, but each person he saw seemed somehow uncertain, as if waiting for another catastrophe to befall their precious world. They glanced furtively left and right, kept their voices down, their manner guarded. That night, Marshall was certain, contingency plans would be laid down. The previous evening had so shattered the calm isolation that was Coudenoure, he wondered if it would ever be as it was again. He ducked into the cottage where he had left Henrietta. Roman enveloped him in a bear hug and sat him before the fire with a cup of tea. Henrietta joined them.

"You, boy . . ." Roman beckoned to a nearby child. "Go and fetch the others, for 'tis a waste to repeat the tale twice."

He ran, and Marshall drank in the silence. He was into his third cup when the others began to filter into the cramped quarters. Rouster was still wiping his hands on a towel thrown over his shoulder; Mary leaned against him comfortably; Henrietta stood behind Roman as he sat; Ben and Elizabeth came together hand in hand, radiating light and youth despite the circumstances. Ian stood alone, red-eyed and unable to shake the shock of his recent loss.

"Now," commanded Roman, "Tell us what you have found."

"Not much that would pass as true intelligence," Marshall began, "But I believe we can make out the pattern."

He set his cup before the fire and pressed on.

"Charles is infatuated with that woman, Alexandra."

Henrietta interrupted him in exasperation.

"We know that!"

"Yes, m'lady, but he conspired with George Villiers - the man who read the King's decree - to get Coudenoure for her."

Roman glared at him.

"And King James? Did he actually approve taking a Baron's lands and estate so that his son's mistress might be satisfied? Eh?" He spit the words rather than spoke them.

Marshall shrugged.

"Where did you get this information?" queried Ben.

"Today, long past sunrise, two horsemen returned to Greenwich. The first was Prince Charles, and we know of his whereabouts last night."

"Indeed." spat Henrietta.

"And the second?" Roman asked.

"The second was an untrustworthy knave by the name of John. He rode in late and I made it my task to care for his mount. In doing so, I asked him where he had been."

A brief pause ensued as he studied their faces and then continued.

"He was angry, and had been hurt in some battle."

A laugh went round and Elizabeth blushed.

"He had ridden with Villiers last evening, and said that Villiers had kidnapped an innocent maid on a pretext of witchery so that Charles' whore could be made happy. He said Villiers had orchestrated it and that the King knew nothing of it."

"I knew it!" Roman shouted. "I shall have my home and family back and by God I shall teach

Villiers what it is to be whipped!" He began pacing but Marshall held up his hand.

"I asked this John how sure he was about King James having no knowledge of the event. In the end, he admitted he had no way of knowing for certain. He also said that, as we all know, the King has a deep and abiding suspicion of women and covens and the like."

Roman sat back down and a silence settled in while these facts were considered. It was Henrietta who spoke first.

"And if we go to the King, we risk being hung should he have been part of the plot. That being said, one of two things must happen before we can reclaim Coudenoure," she said slowly.

Ben offered affirmation.

"Yes. When the King passes, then the threat to you and my Elizabeth being hung as witches dies with him."

Nods of agreement and anticipation ensued on the part of all assembled.

"And the second?" asked Roman.

"The second is that, as we all know, men tire of mistresses." Ian spoke with assurance. "Particularly needy, demanding mistresses."

Roman poked the fire as Ian continued.

"'Tis a mathematical equation: when one side changes, the other must also. When one of those two things occurs, then ye may be certain that the equation will swing and if we are in a position to do so, we can force it to swing our way."

"And in the meantime?" asked Rouster. "We whom she views as servants can continue on and even provide intelligence as to the situation. But what of Henrietta and Roman? Ian? Ben and Elizabeth?"

Ian and Ben coughed at the same moment.

"Elizabeth and I have considered these things already - we came to the same conclusion. It would be best if the number of family scattered across the estate were minimal. I am almost certain that Alexandra will seldom if ever venture out here into the cottages, and therefore for the time being, if Roman and Henrietta could stomach the insult, they would be safe amongst the servants."

"Aye," Rouster nodded enthusiastically at the two. "We can continue to cook for you and Roman, you have always enjoyed going out with the herds. You can continue your crossbreeding while we hunker down and wait this out. And Henrietta, why, you can take up your mother's pursuits in Bess' workshop." He referred to the cottage which years ago had been set up as an artists' space as a suitable place where Bess might pursue her work.

All considered this wordlessly.

Ben coughed again before speaking.

"Elizabeth and I have decided to go to Corpus Christi for the waiting time."

Henrietta stared at him while great tears welled in her eyes.

"Leave? Why would you do that? We are family!"

Elizabeth took up their defense.

"Mama, we will only be at Oxford. We have many friends there now - why, just last weekend was not Coudenoure home to many of them? They have told us to come and be part of their community! Ben has interest in the Bodleian, and I could work with men of science to increase my learning! Mother, no, do not weep. We will be safe, nearby, and when this is over, we will come home, rest assured."

"Child, you have never been outside Coudenoure. Women do not dabble in science else they be called witches." Henrietta's point produced more silence.

"We are going, and if I do nothing more than make a home for Ben, then I am happy."

"Ian?" Roman looked at him.

"I am going home," came his simple reply. "I cannot be here where she was but is no more. I cannot. I will see what is left for me in the north country."

His words were so somber and final that no one questioned him.

"We will have to get behind the mantel in the library once more," Henrietta said thoughtfully, ". . . for these things will require coinage."

"That part is simple," Rouster and Ben spoke together and Marshall laughed.

"Like old times on the streets of London, eh? We shall have no trouble with this small bit of tomfoolery."

And so it was done. The parting of the ways.

Bright and early just before sunrise the next day, three people left Coudenoure for new lives, three continued on as before, and two, shaken to their core, remained as outlaws in their own home, in the cottage on the end of the row nearest to the fields.

Chapter Thirteen

December 1623

There was a light snow. The servant boy had brought in wood and stoked the fire well, but still the chill swirled and eddied in Ian's bones. He stretched lower in the old chair so that his legs and feet, balanced precariously on the small footstool before him, extended well beyond it towards the fire. Ah, there. He wiggled his toes in their threadbare stockings with satisfaction and pulled the old blanket closer round his shoulders. Yes, better, definitely. He turned to glance through the window.

Snowing. Again. Would it ever stop? He held up his hand and for the tenth time that day, bent his fingers forward as he counted off the months until spring.

"That would be January, yes, and February, and March and April . . ."

"Same as last time, old man."

Maggie, the caretaker's wife, appeared from a door recessed in the far reaches of the room. She banged down a tray with tea on the table at his side and commenced pouring him a cup.

"I will tell you what I think." She spoke with the thickest of Scottish brogues.

"Oh, please do." Ian's sarcasm was lost on her.

Aye, then. Ian Hurlbert, what are ye doing, man? Eh? Ye return to Scotland, and I have to ask ye, why, man, why did ye come hither?"

Ian closed his eyes and felt the warmth from the cup pierce his fingers and hands.

"Why, indeed." He knew that his laconic answer would lead to more of everything: of Maggie's sharp tongue, of dead memories of a sorrowful past and of a future with no joy. Maggie's voice cut into his thoughts and proved him right.

"Ye should hear me, old son. Ye are killing yourself with all of this." She poured herself a cup of tea and waved her hand airily about as she sat in the chair opposite his.

She decided to take his lack of response as interest in her prognostications.

"Now when Bruce died, me and the master were heartbroken we were."

She passed Ian a piece of bread with a small bit of ham wrapped within. She made the same for herself before leaning back and continuing.

"When was that, um? Old master says it was the year after the big snow, but I know different. Ye see, I felt stirrings well before that. My heart told me that our boy was not well, and I was proven right. T'was not a fortnight later but he took sick and was gone."

Rather than cheering either of them up or even making a valid, constructive point, Maggie's remembrance began to cast a thin pall of morose sadness over the pair.

"Aye, t'was bad times, they were. And I never told my boy good-bye, ye see, for I was out at market. The old lady – the one who used to live in the cottage behind the first hill there . . ." she paused and pointed towards the window, as though Ian might have missed this detail of Castle Donoway in all his time there, ". . . that crone knew the ways of healing, and she sent me to get what we needed to make Bruce well."

Maggie sipped her tea.

"Aye." She fell silent for a moment.

"But t'was too late, ye see. He was gone."

Ian reached for another piece of bread and more tea.

"I am sorry for your loss, Maggie. But you and Old Master (Ian was not sure he had ever heard the man's Christian name) went on to have other children who bring you joy."

Maggie sighed.

"Aye, but none are the likes of Bruce. He was a golden child, you see, my first and best."

As she shook her head she looked keenly at Ian.

"My point, old man, is that ye must move on. Oh, sure, the sadness will always be there, t'will never leave ye in fact, but ye must harness it to better things or ye will die, ye *will* I say - sad and broken and old and . . ."

"*Thank you,* Maggie, I believe I see the dire future you predict clearly enough."

She nodded, satisfied that she had made progress.

"Why do ye not read some of those books of yours? Um? Or walk to market and meet people instead of roaming (she give the 'r' a particularly hard trill for emphasis) amongst the heather and hills, alone?"

Ian smiled at her and lied.

"Perhaps I will, Maggie. Now, if you do not mind, I need to do some thinking. I can see myself to bed."

Maggie stood and took the tray. As she walked away, Ian heard her clearly.

"*Perhaps I will.* Oh aye, he thinks I do not hear the lie upon his lips. *Perhaps I will* . . . I canna let him die here alone and in the prime of his life yet! T'would be a sin on my soul before God . . ."

Ian smiled in spite of himself. A familiar banging of pots and shouts began from the next room and he settled deeper in his chair.

"Maggie, there is no sin upon you, but upon he who killed my Anne, aye, his sin is beyond measure." He spoke the words to himself. And then, as he did each evening, he closed his eyes and thought of his lost wife.

He did not realize that Maggie, in her own way, was good and truly done with his grief. Early the next morning, she sent William to stoke the fire and give Ian his tea. She rode to the nearby village and sought out the priest, the one amongst them who could read and write. Giving him a penny offering for the plate, she dictated a letter to him. Afterwards, he folded it and addressed it as she commanded. She took it and passed it along to the town crier with another penny to see it safely to his contact in Edinburgh. From there, she said a prayer for it to reach that faraway place the good father had written upon the outside and by noon she was back at Donoway.

*****

Ian would be the first to admit he had never moved beyond Anne's death. She was gone, that much was true, but he yet oriented himself through her. When the crocuses appeared across the march in their brilliant yellow parade, undulating over the great and low landscape of heather and lichens, he knew they also blanketed Quinn's meadow where he and Anne had walked. When bluebells popped through their snowy mantle in the early spring, he could not help but notice how their intense color, their gentle nods, mirrored that of Anne's beloved lavender. And the wild poppies, tall, orange, whimsical, grew in Donoway's abandoned lawn as they did at Coudenoure in Quinn's meadow. He gathered them in small bouquets in her memory, laying them upon the great boulders and outcroppings of the lonely north.

His summers, too, repeated the rhythms of his summers with Anne. There were plants to be discovered and examined, children from the estate to be watched over, observations of moon and stars, remembrances of happy past times with Anne. In the far north, the sun rose early and tarried late in the summer, and he found himself in a happier frame of mind, as he and Anne had done in their time together. But the autumn and winter, aye. Time slowed and bittered like raw greens upon the tongue. He rose late and retired early; he seldom shuffled farther than the distance between his chair, the kitchen area and his bed.

And always, behind it all, despite his best efforts, Ian relived the season leading up to Ben and Elizabeth's wedding day – the day of Anne's murder, in a repeating loop. It did not matter where the tale stood when he closed his eyes at night: the next morning it picked back up where it had left off and played on relentlessly. He marveled at the happy isolation and ignorance of the world beyond Coudenoure's gates that each of them had exhibited in their happy stupor at Coudenoure.

But most of all, Ian relived his inability to save Anne. It was the stain upon his soul he could not wash clean. Had he moved more quickly and stepped in front of her, or if he had engaged the mob before they reached her. Aye. What if. What if he had pulled her behind him and taken the wound himself; what if he had grabbed her hand and pushed her aside or run away or frightened the mobs' horses or or or. What if. He could not rise above it nor could he walk through it. It was the air he breathed, the dreams he dreamt, the world in ashes around him.

Chapter Fourteen

1624

Autumn had returned once more and Maggie urged him to get out, see people, do something. But again Ian had no say in the matter - his heart would not brook resistance to its sorrow and unfathomable grief. Should he have a conversation with someone, anyone, why, he would want to discuss it with Anne. That night in bed, should a guest have stopped by for supper, they would discuss it, turn it round and enjoy it together. He could not do so now, and so he did not set up situations which would remind him further of that angle of his loss. Too much. Too much.

On that particular morning, the snows had not yet begun. A lazy sun beat down upon the browning meadows and fields of Donoway, and Ian dressed for his usual morning walk. His clothes were an odd mix of threadbare breeches and stockings and new cloaks and vests. He ignored the contrast. He used a cane not because of need but because of feeling. He felt an old man and therefore he would use a cane. He was helping himself towards a life of nothing and Maggie was more and more agitated about it.

"So ye will take your sad little stroll through the sad autumn meadows, will ye?"

She spoke with a deliberately perky sarcasm. As always Ian ignored it.

"Tell me, where is my cane?" he asked looking about.

"And how would I be knowing that, eh, old man? Perhaps ye are losing your mind and have lost another one."

Ian knew well that he had not lost the first two canes which had gone missing, nor had he lost this one. He had not misplaced the various vests, cloaks, used-up stockings and toques which could no longer be found. No. Maggie did not like the man he was setting himself up to be and so she got rid of each of his stage props on a routine basis, switching them out for bright and shiny new ones. All, that is, except the cane – those she simply burnt in the kitchen fire. He always asked politely, she always swore no knowledge of their whereabouts.

As he opened the front door, he was surprised to see a horseman picking his way along what used to be the well-graveled drive of the place.

"Maggie, are you expecting someone?"

She moved close and squinted for a better look.

"No," she said quietly. "Now, what do you suppose he wants?"

"We shall find out soon enough," came Ian's puzzled reply. "Make some tea, Maggie, and see if any of those biscuits from last week are still edible."

Maggie disappeared and Ian continued his watch. The man who approached was crisply dressed in fine but local attire. He pulled his mount to a halt before Ian.

"Good day, sire."

Ian nodded.

"I seek Ian Hurlbert. Is this his castle?" The stranger spoke the word cautiously and looked with disbelief at the sight before him, as though even a harsh breath might cause further wreck and ruin to the place.

"I am he. Come in and have tea, please."

"No, aye, I will not trouble ye for such. I have a letter from Edinburgh for ye and have been told to deliver it only into your hands."

Ian held out his hand. The horseman smiled and fumbled ostentatiously in his vest.

"Now where did I put it?" the words flowed innocently from his lips. Finally, Ian tumbled to the situation and excused himself momentarily, reappearing in due course with a small coin.

"Aye, here it is!" The horseman handed it over tipped bowed as he took the coin. Turning without another word, he receded into the distance.

Maggie was back.

"Oh, a letter!"

Ian closed the door and they sat together for tea as he examined it.

"Who would be sending me a letter, um?" he asked absently as Maggie poured their cups. "It says here 'tis from Edinburgh, but below that is yet another place, I believe in England. What do you suppose . . ."

Maggie was up in a flash and disappeared into the kitchen.

A long time later, Ian still sat holding the now open letter and staring at the fire. His tea had gone cold.

Chapter Fifteen

"Perhaps we are peasants, after all."

"I am, but I thought you knew that."

It had become their ritual. Each evening, along with the other laborers and craftsmen of Coudenoure, Henrietta and Roman returned to their small cottage at sunset. While Roman cleaned the fields and the smell of sheep from himself before the fire, Henrietta ladled water for the kettle. She then set it to boil on the three-legged spider which sat within the smaller fireplace in the kitchen area. Eventually, when each had taken a moment to collect themselves, she brought it forward to the main hearth. As they settled into their favorite chairs (purloined as they liked to giggle, from the great lady's house), they took turns recounting their days to one another. The beginning was always the same.

"Who shall speak first, today, um?" Henrietta would ask as she poured. Today was Roman's turn.

"Well, you may not believe it, but I have successfully crossed my Ryeland sheep with those Lincolnshire ewes I bought."

"*No,*" exclaimed Henrietta, as though hearing about it for the first time.

"Indeed." Roman sipped his tea.

"You see, Hen, the purpose of the cross is to bring forward the best of each breed."

"Um-hmm."

"Yes, I wanted the heartiness of the Lincolnshire breed and the fleece of my Ryelanders."

More tea.

"When my father was alive, we considered this. Our hope was as mine – to have the softest yet most durable wool. We tried many crosses."

"I recall that – what was the outcome, my love?"

And off Roman would go, describing the various crosses he and his father had attempted. This, in turn, always led to a discussion of Roman's father and background.

"My father was an amazing, man."

"Roman, he was indeed, as are you."

More tea.

"He began life on the Spencer estate, Althorp, as a tenant farmer."

"Um."

"How he managed to have the industry to shed that life and become part of the larger world of wool and cloth is quite extraordinary."

"Indeed."

"He had a seat on the wool exchange by the age of forty. Forty! Can you imagine? And we still own the lot, you know, where their house was."

"Aye," Henrietta would interject sympathetically, ". . . the fire was a great tragedy - your parents would be with us still today were it not for that."

They both mused a few moments upon memories of the past, sad and sweet.

"Perhaps we should rebuild on it one day. It might be nice to have a home in the city, do you not think so?"

Henrietta always laughed at this point.

"Dear, we are barely managing to have a home in the country! Fie! I think the notion of city-dwelling should wait a generation or two, do not you agree?"

Roman would always utter a jovial agreement and the conversation would turn to Henrietta's day.

"And you, my dear wife? Your day?"

"Well, you may not believe it . . ." Henrietta's lead-in always mirrored Roman's, ". . . but I believe I have found a way to work the stone around the dark vein which permeates it."

"Indeed."

More tea.

"Yes. You see, I understand now that is why mother must have put this particular slab of marble aside. She knew of the flaw and therefore wanted to consider it from all sides before assigning it to a particular work."

"Your mother was very smart, Hen. I am sure you are right."

"Well. When I began following her example I did not understand such matters. Why, after my first sculpture, I was so eager for another that I assumed she was holding this piece for something special - now I know!"

"We miss her, do we not?"

Henrietta always rejoined in the same fashion, discussing her mother as Roman had his father.

"Yes. Roman, did you know that her mother, Constance, traveled to Italy, knew Michelangelo? Our lore has always been that Bess was his daughter. That would account for my attraction to art and my abilities with stone. It is as though I have been waiting my entire life for the moment I first picked up my chisel and hammer."

At this juncture, the tea would have grown cold, and Roman would take up Henrietta's initial comment which had opened their evening's ritual.

"Perhaps we are peasants after all."

He would reach for Hen's hand.

She would squeeze his in return, and always reply, "How else to account for such contentment in our present state? Um?"

There was time, and room, for discussion of other things. Was the orchard bearing fruit this year; what had the seamstress been thinking when she sewed pants and leggings for the estate's children: each pair had room for two; had there been word from Elizabeth and Ben in Oxford? So many things they could talk about.

But they did not. There was no fear of broadening their world, but rather a cautious acknowledgement that they simply chose not to. It was as if that fateful day had never happened; like some unspeakable evil, it was locked away in a strongbox deep within their souls, lest further trouble bloom in the small patch of sunshine they had managed to salvage. To bring it forth would be to give it life. Anne's murder, the loss of the estate, the emptiness which settled in upon them with the departure of Ben and Elizabeth and Ian . . . no. This way, their way, was better.

But at odd moments, each of them could be caught unawares by the powerful memories of their past. Henrietta might see a child running in the meadow, and gasp - how the little boy looked like Thomas! Or perhaps white strawberry locks floating behind some little girl as she chased her friends down the allee - why, that was Elizabeth, surely! A Greek phrase in a book, a note in a scribbled birdlike hand, a whiff of fresh lavender - almost anything could bring Anne rushing back to her, never gone, breaking her heart all over again. Her heart never sobbed for the luxury of the manor house with its grand rooms and fine furnishings and rugs and books; only for those no longer with her did it bleed.

As for Roman, he frequently sat beneath the elm in the back field while the sheep grazed. How far could a man fall, he wondered. He never talked of his own youth, flagrantly misguided, lost save for the love given him by his parents and Henrietta. Henrietta - he thought of their unbelievable escape from the Tower, of Queen Elizabeth's gracious acceptance of him and his family. Frequently, he laughed aloud as he remembered his clumsy attempts at courtly, refined behavior when he had met her. How bored she must have been with his tales of wool and broadcloth and the trade with Spain! And flax! Why the French linen trade was wreaking havoc with English wool! Did she not understand that wool was the primary export of England, had been for centuries? But she had understood, she did know, but she had chosen not to make him feel small with her own wide knowledge of the trade.

Sometimes, when he closed his eyes, he saw Thomas running to him up the hill across the stream. In his mind, Thomas was always the tow-headed little one who held Roman's heart in his small hands. Ah, who knew a heart could ache for so long. He did not miss Ben and Elizabeth for they sent notes through various backchannels of their doings. They brought first their one child, then their second, each Christmas to visit Hen and him. There was great joy at those times.

Roman, though, was a man of action. He needed resolution to their current situation. He should arrange a visit with Prince Charles or slay Villiers or demand an audience with King James himself. But he knew he could not, for the price of resolution might be not Coudenoure, but the lives of Henrietta and Elizabeth. They had been branded as witches by the King himself. Villiers' claimed to have read a writ from James' own hand demanding they be turned over for a fate too ghastly even to consider. As it had come upon them, though, so it had vanished. In the early days after Elizabeth's rescue, all of Coudenoure shivered in anticipation of what was surely yet to come. Contingency plans, children left with far-away relatives, food stores and horses hidden away - that had been their lives for many months. Patterns began to emerge, however, and they were encouraging. Alexandra seldom left her new manor house, and when she did, she did not venture into the allee of cottages which housed her servants and craftsmen. And Hen and Roman. The panic of that night slowly began to ratchet down. The days distilled themselves into two major events: when the Prince would visit, and when 'Papa' would visit. They were never at Coudenoure at the same time, and the few times they might have met had seen 'Papa' pulling on his vest and boots hurriedly as he scampered (if a middle-aged man can do so) out the back way to fetch his horse from the stable. Early on he had learned the back way to and from Greenwich.

Coudenoure had slowly stabilized, and with that easing of consternation came the realization that so long as Alexandra's needs were met, they were safe. No one really understood that fateful night but all gave thanks that Coudenoure still functioned as home and hearth for their small community.

Sometimes at night, Roman awoke in a cold sweat, having dreamt the only dream he ever remembered upon waking. He was in the chapel ruins and the mob was there. They threw themselves at Henrietta and Elizabeth and fought through the crowd to reach them. He wanted to help, he needed to save them. But his feet would not move. They were grown into the earth like ancient oaks. He screamed out for them to run but he was frozen. Unable to save those who had saved him with their love and nurture. Henrietta would wake him, hold him until the sweats subsided and he returned to a fitful sleep. But never did she ask what the nightmare was about and never did he volunteer.

Roman and Henrietta set off down the only path open to them after that terrible evening of Anne's murder and the marriage of Ben and Elizabeth. They had not strayed and as a result their behavior was fossilized, embedded now in the weave of their past. Neither wanted to jolt the other into painful memories; neither chose to talk of their own. Occasionally, when a laugh between them brought a shared remembrance they could see the need in one another's eyes: talk would have been good, may have helped to heal the gaping wounds. But they could not, and the more time passed the more confident their belief in and dependence upon their ritual grew. They could shut it all out, be happy in their cottage, with one another.

A knock on the door came as it did each evening and Roman shouted entry.

"Oh aye, now, I am not interrupting you, am I?"

And there would be Rouster with a tray in one hand and a bit of ale in the other. He would put away the tea and replace it with dinner. As they ate, he stoked the fire and told them of the day's jibber jabber from the estate.

Did they know that Prince Charles had turned up today? Um? T'was his first visit in some time, perhaps a year even, and there had been a serious row in the library. Mary believed he was tiring of the whore. What did they think? How was the roast beef? Cooked to their satisfaction? Here, let me pour you some ale. He was mindful always of what Henrietta and Roman had done for him and therefore for his family. He gave them respect, even now that they lived in the last cottage behind the manor house of Coudenoure.

As he walked back to the manor kitchen each night, the lights in the kitchen were still ablaze, for Mary always waited up for him, saw him safely home.

Chapter Sixteen

"Pull it tighter!" she sucked in her breath and pushed her shoulders back. "Tighter!"

Annabelle, her ladies' maid, attempted to cinch the laces tighter. She was beginning to consider a system of ropes and pulleys to help her - or perhaps a team of oxen - when she caught Alexandra's furious gaze. She looked down and focused on her nigh impossible task.

They stood before the looking glass in the bedchamber, and Alexandra glared through its shimmery mercury finish at Annabelle who strained and sweated valiantly behind her.

"Madame . . ." the girl began with a deeply respectful gasp.

"Mademois*elle*," . . . Alexandra gasped in return, "I am a *maiden*! Why must I continuously remind you of that fact?"

"Because Mama says you cannot be both a common tart *and* a maid?"

Alexandra swirled round to see who dared speak such blasphemy. A small tot, no more than four, sat complacently on the floor beside Annabelle, eating an apple and watching the struggle with wide-eyed curiosity. A swift kick from Annabelle sent the little one scurrying from the room, and the two women returned to the battle at hand.

Alexandra needed to look her best today, for notice had come from Greenwich that Prince Charles would visit Coudenoure in the afternoon. It was good that such advance notice had arrived. Otherwise she would have pummeled and possibly maimed him on sight. Annabelle was finally sent to retrieve her best gown – the burgundy silk which accentuated her dark eyes and olive skin. Two sheets of identical silk had been sewn as slim panels onto each side of the bodice's back seam. As she waited impatiently she turned this way and that before the mirror, smiling at the plan she had devised; well, not so much a plan as an act of raw retribution.

Charles had not visited in well over a year. Initially, believing the prince simply busy with state affairs, Alexandra had spent her days familiarizing herself with Coudenoure. It was small relative to other manor homes she had visited with the court retinue, but jewel-like in its symmetry and beauty. Its scale was strange yet magnetically appealing.

Upon entrance into the main hall, one was swept up in the sheer height of the room. It took a moment to scale back one's view and begin to see the priceless, aged artifacts that adorned its floors and walls. Flemish tapestries, rich in detail and huge, hung upon the walls. Busts of the purest marble graced tables while gleaming bronze sconces with intricate designs flung light across the darkened room. Rugs from far-away lands, tightly woven with intricate patterns covered the huge limestone blocks of the floor. One of them had caused much curiosity on Alexandra's part: she had seen it before. As the months passed, her irritation with herself and the rug grew, only resolved by happenstance - she stumbled across a rough depiction of it in one of the books in her new library. Hans Memling had apparently used it as a backdrop in one of his paintings. This pleased her mightily.

Moving from the great entryway into the library, there was nothing to be seen but the vast collection of books, which she now owned. Upon her first visit to Coudenoure, she had declared carelessly that she would burn or sell them all. Whether she had meant those harsh and ignorant words she could not remember, but regardless, her feelings had changed. After the discovery about the rug in the hallway, she had become entranced with the library, not for its own value (which was considerable), but for what it might tell her of her new belongings. Her inability to read was an intense barrier to understanding her newfound treasure, and she set about finding a remedy.

Claiming only to want to understand the common people who now worked for her, she employed Annabelle to give her lessons in the written word. From there she had begun to employ the girl as a ladies' maid, for despite having gifted her with Coudenoure, Charles had not seen fit to provide her with court servants: she was dependent upon those already at Coudenoure.

Alexandra's growing expertise had a strange effect on her, one she not anticipated. She had always viewed it as a skill for lesser beings, which in her mind meant those born without physical beauty. What need had a woman such as herself, a rare creature, for such a pedantic and boring skill? That changed the moment she read her first word. What had seemed a somewhat trivial pursuit - perhaps she would show off her new skill to Charles upon his next visit - became a ravenous thirst for words, and meaning and knowledge. For the first time in her life, she was exploring something beyond herself and her relationship with men. Her survival in a man's world had always been dependent upon her beauty. But this took her far beyond that realm. No man controlled it nor was a man able to dictate her behavior concerning it. It moved from novel to necessary, from frivolous to freedom to passion almost overnight.

She determined that nothing less than fluency in the written word would please her. But while she had begun her quest to read as a means of understanding her belongings, she continued it for the raw pleasure, and real power, it gave her. But she did not anticipate what else it might reveal.

It had happened during one of her reading sessions - she was taking her tea at a small table she had placed on the wide gravel sweep that fronted Coudenoure between the house and Quinn's Meadow. A clip-clop at the far end of the drive alerted her to company, and she watched as a man on horseback plodded to a halt before her. He bowed and pulled a satchel forward from his side.

"Is this Coudenoure?" he inquired politely.

"Of course it is! Can you not read - the name is on the gate!" Alexandra was pleased with her snide remark.

The courier ignored her and produced a sealed paper from the bag.

"This is for Baron de Gray, Roman Collins."

Alexandra was standing now and reached imperiously for the page.

"I shall take it. The baron is no longer in residence here."

The man pulled it just out of her reach.

"I am instructed to place it in his hands, Madame."

"Madem-*moiselle.*"

She did not catch the hooded doubting look he cast in her direction. Again she reached for the paper. Reluctantly he passed it to her.

"I will see to this," she assured him.

"You will give it to the Baron?"

"Um? Yes, of course. Whatever."

He waited politely in the saddle. His horse did not move. She realized he waited for some small token of appreciation.

"Be gone, man." She stepped forward and waved her arms, startling the horse. "I have nothing for you."

The man glared, turned, and clip-clopped back down the drive, disappearing in the direction from whence he had come. She thought she heard the words, "mademoiselle my arse," but she could not be certain.

Settling once more into her chair, she poured a cup of tea and inspected the letter. It was thrilling to be able to read the salutation and address:

Roman Collins

Baron de Grey of Coudenoure

Coudenoure

There was no hesitation as she broke its seal - after all, she was now the mistress of Coudenoure and surely the letter pertained to issues about her estate. With tea in one hand and letter in the other she began reading:

My dear Roman,

I hope this finds you and Henrietta well. I heard there was a spot of trouble at Coudenoure but that it soon passed. Let me know if this news is in error, or if I should come to your rescue! What a sight that would be!

Alexandra snorted, wondering what . . . here she looked down the page to the signature . . . Alford de Garney, must look like since the sight of him rescuing 'Roman' would be so amusing. She found her place and on she went:

I am afraid I write of bad news concerning the price of wool this year. The exchange has practically shut down, for all about men and estates are waiting for better prices. Aye, Roman, but they are not coming. There are many who beg in the streets now, and I fear the worst.

But let me move on to brighter subjects. I hear

Prince Charles has gone abroad – to Spain of all places – seeking a bride . . ."

The porcelain tea cup hit the gravel.

I am told that the good Duke of Buckingham (George Villiers) sails with him, so we may be assured that our sovereign will be successful in his pursuit of a bride. Our England needs an heir and Prince Charles is seeing to it!

I must tell you now of Dolly and our newest child, Emily.

Alexandra had never felt such intense burning anger as she did now. So he would throw her away! HER! ALEXANDRA OF MALTA tossed aside like some pale, vapid, wan, pale, vapid . . . she could not think of words fast enough and ended up just repeating the same ones over and over. Vapid, wan, pale, stupid . . . English woman. No! No! Not even that! A Spaniard yet! It was too much to bear.

The servant girl appeared with a kettle to warm the pot on the table. Alexandra grabbed it from her, threw it as hard as she could into the meadow, and howled like a wolf on a moonlit night. The servant screamed in terror and ran. The table was next – into the meadow and farther than the kettle even. The screaming and pacing went on for some time. Finally, Rouster appeared hesitantly at the doors to the manor house. Bowing and scraping, he made his way towards the roaring pacing conflagration that was Alexandra.

"Madame . . .."

"*MADEMOISELLE!!!* AAARRRGGGHHH!" She kicked the chair out of her way and disappeared into the house and up the stairs. The screaming continued but she had switched to her native tongue, reaching for additional words to describe Charles - English, it seems, fell short in this area. A distant door slamming put an end to it, and both Mary and Rouster advised the estate's children to play outside for the day.

*****

From that day until now, Alexandra had lain in wait for Prince Charles with only bonbons and candied fruit to look forward to each day. But the silk panels were barely noticeable, and as Annabelle held the gown low and Alexandra stepped into it, she was in awe, as she always was, of the ability of a good gown to make a woman feel better. Carriage wheels could be heard upon the drive; with a splash of rose water she went down to greet the Prince.

Chapter Seventeen

The dynamic was not there. Time and again during that afternoon, Alexandra had plied her wares to no avail. She batted her coal-lined ebony eyes coyly . . . Prince Charles continued eating jam pennies; she leaned forward so that he might have a better view . . . he told her of the two new hats he had ordered from Rome; she leaned back and curled her finger through a lock of hair . . . he took his shoes off like an old man before a comfortable and warm fire. It was pointless. And then, as she mentally thrashed about seeking how best to entrap the twit so that she might have the upper hand, Charles did the unthinkable. She had kept her knowledge of his trip abroad in abeyance, planning to spring it upon him when he least expected it and when she could most deploy it to her advantage. But it did not transpire in that manner.

"Tell me, my Prince, why have you been away so long?" An artful pout formed upon her perfect lips.

"Well, I must tell you, my father is quite ill, as you know."

"Yeeessss," she purred. Perhaps the letter had been wrong, and he was here to propose!

"As heir to the throne, I feel the weight of the kingdom upon my shoulders in ever increasing amounts."

"'Tis difficult for one as sensitive as you, my Lord."

"Um, indeed. So I went to Spain to seek a bride!"

It took a moment.

"What did you say, my love?"

Prince Charles was oblivious to the warning signs - Alexandra now sat straight as a door jamb. Her lips had thinned to fine lines of ink on a manuscript's page. Her complexion paled to a dull and sallow hue. But Charles went gaily forward with what he believed to be a amusing tale of his and George Villiers' exploits.

"Yes, you see Buckingham and I both believed that the Spanish Infanta Maria Anna would be an excellent match for me, and therefore for England!"

It was fortunate that Charles turned his head in time to see the vase flying his way. As he ducked, Alexandra hurled its mate with even more fury.

"Buckingham? Is he now your *bawd*?" Alexandra swept round upon him, ". . . you, you fenny, festering fainéant of a rake."

"My dear, your vocabulary has grown greatly in my absence!"

"Get out!!"

"I beg your pardon?" Charles was still clueless as to his sin but even he could not fail to read the explosive anger which roiled the room at this point.

"You think you may come here and tell me of your search for a bride? What about me? I should be your bride! I *will* be your bride!"

A scraping sound from the wall which separated the library from the great hall went unnoticed. There, Rouster and Mary stepped back from where they had plastered their ears to the limestone. Rouster carefully replaced a piece of mortar between the stones, mortar which had been thus replaced and removed for centuries, as evidenced by the smooth dip in the stone floor just beneath it.

"Aye, 'tis still the best listening post in the kingdom," Rouster grinned.

"Quickly, we must go about our business - we will discuss their brawl this evening."

Mary and he went their separate ways.

Late that night, as they curled together in the bedchamber just off the kitchen, they giggled like schoolchildren about the quarrel. They seldom used the cottage assigned to them, for the simple reason that they were pleased with their current set-up. Their four children slept in the bed adjacent to theirs. Others might have spurned such an arrangement, but they loved it. That night, Annabelle, their eldest, had told them of Alexandra's great anticipation of the Prince's arrival. As the night gave way to the deep unconcerned breathing of their children asleep, they discussed it.

"What do you suppose it means?" Rouster whispered. "Is she out of favor and if so, what will happen?"

"I do not know," his wife mused as they cuddled deeper under the covers, "I think we should bring it up, I do, this year upon the ridge. What do you think, husband?"

"Aye, Mary, you are right. And 'tis only a few nights hence. Ben and Marshall will know what to do."

They faded into a happy, single dream.

Chapter Eighteen

The Romans had come and had conquered the heathen land to the north. Caesar ruled and after him, in the deep mists of the dark times, had ridden Arthur, Merlin at his side casting spells and conjuring nature itself into complicity with his wishes. Aye, Uther Pendragon and Igraine. Lancelot and Guinevere, Mordred. Peace's end at Avalon. But their day faded, their heroics all but leached from history by the darkness which settled in upon the land. For centuries, knowledge bled from the shores of England.

But time had moved on, and slowly, imperceptibly, light crept across the broad sky once again, seeping in between the dark lichens and mosses laid down by the ages. And northwest of Londinium arose a community of monks and of scholars. Built upon the ancient ford of the Thames River used to drive oxen to and from market, it took the name Oxford and grew to a village. Within its walls, aularian communities sprang up and gave life to a university, the oldest in the kingdom. Oxford.

It was to Oxford that Elizabeth and Ben fled in the early dawn hours of that mournful December day in 1620. By that year, the university was already ancient and steeped in lore. It harbored within its halls and chapels and churches and libraries all the knowledge that had been salvaged by the realm from the Dark Ages. Its denizens kept bold watch over the ephemera and scraps of papyrus and vellum, books and scrolls that told of the deep past; the entire community kept zealous faith with the ancients.

There had been no time to notify their friends in Oxford, the scholars with whom they routinely corresponded, of their predicament. In the night preceding their flight, they had crept one last time into the manor house of Coudenoure and taken from it the family's treasure of coin. It was considerable, and what they and Ian did not need was buried in the floor of Henrietta's and Roman's new home, their cottage. Horses and tack were waiting for them on the far side of Coudenoure's fields, and with a final hug they were gone to a new life. Their clothes were those of craftsmen, their saddles the oldest and most worn on the estate. It would do no good to draw attention to themselves, and they rode sedately, blending in with the throngs traveling to London with their wares.

Once beyond the crowds on the far side of London, they veered northwest and in few days time had made Oxford. Ben had routinely visited the university, always seeking manuscripts and scrolls, and they quickly found their way to a friend's home. It was with surprise that John Beddow opened his door to find the two of them standing on his stoop.

"God's knees!"

"Not quite," came Ben's dry reply. "Just two weary refugees in need of sanctuary."

The tone in Ben's voice, the dark purple shadows beneath Elizabeth's eyes, the state of their horses behind them, all spoke to an urgent desperation on their part. Beddow stood aside and they passed beneath the portal silently. After a moment, a houseboy went out, collected their mounts and disappeared down the street.

They stood in a room no bigger than the entry hall of Coudenoure. A low fire burned within a small hearth surrounded by several deep chairs. A table near the front window was piled high with paper, inkwells, quills and books. On top of it all was a blanket which Beddow had evidently thrown off when they had knocked upon his door. The fire seemed to do kitchen duty as well, for various pots hung from its mantel and jars of kitchen wares and grains sat upon the same. Like peas in a pod, three neat, identical doors opened off the back wall. Through one could be glimpsed an unmade bed, another sported a view of books piled hither and thither against walls and in cases, and the third was closed. The walls were bare, the room lit by two enormous candles which burned on either side of the fireplace.

Their host busied himself with ladling water from a nearby jug into a pot, which sat on a neat pile of bricks just within the fire's reach. All the while he kept up a running dialogue, mostly with himself; Elizabeth took him in as he did so.

"Well! 'Tis a surprise to see you! You look quite worn and I believe strong tea is necessary."

He was short, and the adjective which repeated itself over and over in Elizabeth's mind was . . . round. His bald head was a perfectly shaped ball. It matched his round, large, owlish eyes, which, in turn, were surrounded by circular tortoise-shell rimmed spectacles.

"'Tis wonderful you are here, for just today I came across a bit of grammar which is quite vexing."

His nose was small and puggishly round. His round chest reminded her of the barrels at Coudenoure used to store food for the winter months. His feet were small and disappeared completely into his fuzzy woolen house shoes.

"Now, Sappho is written in the Aeolic dialect, but would you believe it - in Homer no less! - I have found a verbal form I believe to be *Aeolic*! Aye! Of course, that cannot be correct, for Homer is Ionic, but I tell you my friend, I suspect the root form is the same! Imagine! You must give me your opinion!"

He puttered about the fire as he continued.

"Aye, quite the mystery. Now, here we go, onto the bricks as I like to say – it will be warm in no time."

But even as she noted the peculiar circularity of his being, she realized that this was not his most notable characteristic. He was kind. She was certain of it.

"Let me see. Cups. Yes, I have two here that I believe will do. John, you must get more," he fussed at himself. "Unfortunately, the cat has got the last of the cream – she is not feeling well, you see."

A tiny dish of milk sat on the floor nearby, evidently for the aged cat, which slumbered on a pile of warm rags set thoughtfully on the hearth for just that purpose. A small basket of jams and biscuits tied with a pretty ribbon waited near the front door to be delivered when next he was out.

Disappearing into the bedchamber, all the while mumbling to himself about the cat (her name was Caroline apparently) he eventually returned with two worn blankets and for the first time addressed Elizabeth and Ben.

"Well, do not just stand there, friends, but be seated."

They did as they were told.

"Here is a bit of cheese and two bits of bread."

They took it gratefully, but were still silent. As she sank into a chair, Elizabeth felt her bones sag to the bottom of her soul. Almost done in with fatigue and disorientation, she had to smile to herself inwardly. She had always wanted to travel, to see the world beyond Coudenoure, but to do it all in a few short days and nights and in such a manner was not what she had envisioned. Ben sat beside her and after more fussing, Beddow supplied them with more bread, cheese and tea.

As they ate, he mused to himself, observing them. Clearly, the woman was Elizabeth, the one Ben had written of. Why, John realized, the date of marriage Ben had mentioned was only a few days ago, so they were newly married! And yet both looked as though all joy had been drained away. He said as much but still neither of his guests responded.

"My friends, what is this?" he asked again. His voice was gentle.

Elizabeth closed her eyes as Ben began to tell their tale. She had thought she would listen as he spoke, but the tea, the bread and cheese, the warmth from the fire, all nibbled away at her resistance to sleep.

An hour later, Ben woke her.

"Come, wife, John has a room for us."

Beddow took one of the stout candles, opened the third door, and they followed him up the narrow staircase behind it. The second floor was identical in layout to the first: a room with a hearth and two smaller ones which opened off of it. Woolen blankets were found and with a somber nod John disappeared back down the stairway. Elizabeth was asleep again before Ben had even arranged their covers.

Chapter Nineteen

Even now, when no signs of persecution or pursuit by royal forces were evident, Elizabeth would awake in a cold sweat screaming. Sometimes it was Anne she cried out to warn; other times her mother. The details of the nightmare varied but the gist remained the same: run, run, run.

Upon their relocation to Oxford, it had been months before she dared venture out. And then the children changed everything. Colleen came along first, further delaying her contact with the world beyond her front door and Coudenoure. Gabriella followed close behind her sister. When she and Ben had been at Oxford some years before, Elizabeth had done more than play with children in the grassy park behind the house. Now she was content to wait it out, whatever 'it' might prove to be. The King was old and would take his warped views of women with him to the grave. Until then, she cleaned the house, cooked, and acquainted herself with the domestic side of life. She had not been shielded from it at Coudenoure by her title and status, but had simply not paid attention. When hungry, Rouster and Mary were always in the kitchen and would sit her in front of the great fire with a treat or an early tea. Her interests had always been in the natural world and the artistic boundary where it collided with books and knowledge. In Oxford, domesticity was new and invigorating, challenging and fun. For a while.

But children grow, and as the girls toddled, then walked, then ran, Elizabeth found herself in need of intellectual activity. Her need coincided with the passage of time, and she and Ben hired a nurse for the girls. Finally, Elizabeth stepped out into the world of Oxford - and with excitement.

But the rare nature of Coudenoure and of her own upbringing was evident from the moment she walked into Corpus Christi. It was a world without women, filled with scholars - yes - but only learned males. They were suspicious of her and her learning, her eagerness to explore. She in turn found them inexplicably closed to her inquiries and conversation. How she missed Coudenoure!

A deep wariness unfamiliar to her soul settled upon her and colored everything in her new world.

Ben understood, had known the world beyond Coudenoure for what it was. Elizabeth never failed to be stunned and put off by it. It was now that they began to refer to their time away as the diaspora, and despite the intellectual stimulation of their surroundings, their longing for home intensified as the years rolled by.

Chapter Twenty

1629

"Colleen! Where is your sister?" Elizabeth called out to the child who came tripping down the narrow stairway.

"Colleen! Did you not hear me?"

"Yes, Mamma, but you see, Gabriella is tied up so she is unable to join us. I will have to eat her supper."

Ben winked at Elizabeth and responded to Colleen.

"Tell me, young one, who tied Gabriella in knots, um?"

Hard thinking was evident by the squint of Colleen's face.

"Well, you see, an ogre, quite a large one, came in and did it. T'was very sad."

"Aye, 'tis too bad. We are having lamb's liver for supper so you must eat hers and yours. Well, I am sure it is for the best."

A concerned look crossed Colleen's face and her parents could see her working something out.

"'Tis not a problem, Papa, for since Gabriella is tied up, I will give her mine. Yes, that is it. She may have my liver and I will have her cream and bread."

The door opened and John Beddow entered. Elizabeth went to find Gabriella.

"Come, John, supper is upon the table."

Together, the five of them sat. Colleen and Gabriella avoided the liver - Colleen because she detested it; Gabriella because Colleen did. Afterwards, as always, the girls settled in upon the knees of Beddow and he read to them from whatever was at hand. The reading was always embellished with ogres, monsters, princesses and fairies. Afterwards, Ben tucked them in their bed upstairs and upon his return civilized conversation ensued.

Until Elizabeth and Ben had knocked upon his door nine years earlier, John Beddow had led a solitary life. His house was adjacent to Corpus Christi College, one of Oxford University's colleges. His father had come to Oxford, to Corpus Christi, in 1571 as a grammarian. The elder John had purchased the house in which the younger now lived. Like his father, he taught in the College. Like his father before him, the ancient Greek world was more real to him than Oxford.

Books, libraries, languages – these were his life. They were his wife and children, his kith and kin. With the passing of his parents, he was left alone in the world. But it did not bother him – in fact, he would have been surprised to know that was the view the world held of him: alone and bookish and therefore sad. The former was true, the latter ridiculous. He was the happiest of souls.

Over time, he had abandoned the upstairs of the place for the simple reason he had no need of it. As a solitary and scholarly individual, the three lower rooms were more than adequate to meet his requirements. When Ben and Elizabeth had arrived, the second story was the obvious solution to their needs. They paid a small rent each month which allowed John to purchase still more books and acquire a second cat, a rare breed with blue eyes and a lovely beige coat.

In quick succession, Colleen and Gabriella had come along, and John began to take his meals with the family. It was altogether a successful arrangement – John and his books; Elizabeth and her science; Ben at the Balliol and teaching at Corpus Christi. In the library there, he had discovered a work donated by Cotton, a copy of an early geography by Dionysius Periegetes. It was startling in its detail, and purported to be a treatise on the known geographical boundaries of the third century. In their spare time, John, Elizabeth and he all worked upon an English translation of the rare text.

That evening, as Ben made tea and the three conversed, John snapped his fingers.

"God in heaven! I almost forgot! A letter arrived today from Coudenoure!" He fished in the several pockets of his vest until he found it and passed it over to Elizabeth.

It was not the usual epistle from home - the outer edges were worn and several locations had been written and crossed out upon its surface with only their place of residence in Oxford not having been struck. She opened it and began reading.

"What is it?" Ben and John asked in unison.

Elizabeth held up her hand for silence until she had finished.

"'Tis from Donoway."

"Where?"

"Donoway, a castle in Scotland which is in our family. It concerns Ian."

She passed it to Ben who read aloud.

"To those at Coudenoure, the home of Ian Hurlbert, this letter concerns him.

"It is dictated by Maggie, his housekeeper, to me, the priest of St. Agnes' Parish."

Ben gave a small laugh as he read ahead down the page.

"Ye must cum at once, for Ian, I tell ye, Ian is killing himself."

"What?"

"The man is forlorn yet about his wife. Aye, he never leaves the house and I am at my wit's ends. Ye must come at once and rescue the poor devil from himself. He walks about with a cane as though he is ancient. Aye, 'tis sad sad sad."

A note from the priest:

"Maggie insists that I write it thrice for emphasis."

'Ye must come! At once!"

Maggie"

It was several days before they determined upon the appropriate response. They understood Ian well enough to know that once he settled into a routine, he was unlikely to vary from it. To save him, from, as Maggie put it, himself, they would have to be clever. In the end, however, it was not cleverness, but love that moved him. Elizabeth composed the letter they believed would bring him home, and it was sent off to Donoway with explicit instructions for haste.

Chapter Twenty-One

Marshall rode alone through the twilight wood of Greenwich. The winter solstice pulled the sun beneath the horizon with both hands, leaving barely enough light for his horse to pick its way along the faded path. He had no need to ask how Prince Charles' affair with the Lady Alexandra advanced. The undisturbed forest floor beneath, deep in leaves and rot, told the tale clearly enough: no one had trod this way for some time. The silence of the place was thick and ghostly - night creatures were not yet about on their patrols; day creatures had retired to the safety of their lairs. Only Marshall and his horse disturbed the primeval quiet that pervaded the dusk.

It was Christmas day, and he was on his way to Coudenoure. Bags filled with wooden soldiers and dolls, fig cakes and ribbons, hair combs and fancy brushes festooned his saddle. Uncle Marshall's arrival was always highly anticipated - he was a reliable source of excellent goodies and gifts. He passed this way every year, for Christmas at Coudenoure had become a ritual imbued with deep significance. It was celebrated by those who had survived the wedding of Ben and Elizabeth, by those who remembered Anne and missed Ian, by those whose loss of Coudenoure still bit and nipped at their souls. The celebration was always upon the ridge, far from the reach of Alexandra and in the place that Ben, Rouster and Marshall had as children called their own. Like a Seder, the supper celebration began with remembrance and hope; and like a Seder, it ended with family and place.

Had it really been only five years since Villiers and his men violated Coudenoure and taken Elizabeth? Since Alexandra had taken up residence as the new owner of the estate? The world had turned upside down in that time, and Marshall tightened his cloak about him as he let his memories run wild of a world now destroyed.

At length he reached the field adjacent to the high ridge that separated Coudenoure from the King's lands, and as his horse stepped into what was left of the day's light, he kicked it into a steady trot. In no time, he had made the path by the river and begun the ascent up the ridge. He was the first to arrive there, and looped his reins over the hitching post built years ago. On the far end of the crest still stood the stone signal station built during the time of the Spanish Armada. It was part of a series of such places along high points stretching from the southern coast of England into the very heart of the kingdom. When the armada had cleared the sea fog which banked against the French coast that August of 1588, when it had showed itself come to destroy England, each station had lit a great fire and like flames upon oil the silent alarum had leapt from one hill to the next crying out its warning across the land.

Near the mid-point of the crest was a long wooden table with rough benches on either side. Adjacent to it was a fire pit, built long after the signal station had been erected. It was to this circular, charred area that Marshall proceeded. He gathered a bit of dry scrub and squatted near its edge. From a belt around his waist, he untied a small tinder kit and from one section of the compact box pulled a small piece of flint, from another a piece of steel. Finally, a third compartment revealed a bit of charred cloth. Placing the cloth atop the kindling, Marshall repeatedly struck the steel with the flint's edge. A shower of sparks rained down upon the cloth and kindling bringing it to life. Marshall commenced adding bits and twigs to his burning creation and did not hear the approaching footsteps.

"Old son." The voice floated on the night air.

Marshall turned and stood. Before him was Roman. He wanted to run to him, embrace him and channel all the strength and energy in the world into his thin frame; he wanted to ask the man before him what had happened, where was his friend and mentor, for surely this could not be the same man he had seen only twelve months earlier. No, that man had been vital, hopeful, upright and full of life. The shell before him, gray and bent, could not be the same man. But as Roman advanced and hugged him mightily, Marshall felt the pulse of life which surged yet through the older man's bones. His hollow cheeks belied the strength that still lay within, the steel core which even tragedy could not touch.

"Oh, aye, and here is Marshall!" It was Henrietta, round and happy and patting Roman on the arm as though checking on him, keeping him safe. Her smiling face almost hid her fierce determination to watch over him and protect him from further pain.

A happy swell of children began tumbling over the far edge of the crest and behind them came Rouster and Mary.

"Careful now. I said careful!" Rouster spoke sharply to a line of scullery maids and kitchen staff who followed behind him, each laden with baskets of food. Bringing up the rear were Ben and Elizabeth.

The celebration had begun.

Chapter Twenty-Two

It was late when Alexandra rang her little bell for service from the kitchen. She preferred her meals in the large room that stood opposite the library, across from the great hall and opening onto it. There, in isolated splendor, with the best candles lit and the finest service laid upon the linen-draped table, she ate alone.

The door from the kitchen opened and Annabelle, her ladies' maid appeared. She pushed a trolley laden with porcelain serving dishes steaming with all manner of Christmas delights.

"Why are you serving me supper?" Alexandra's voice was thick with ale and boredom. "Where is my kitchen staff?"

"Oh, m' lady, there is a terrible ailment sweeping through the servants' quarters. I alone seem immune to it and so I volunteered to serve your grace, so as not to endanger you."

The lie flowed lightly as Annabelle placed the various dishes on the table before Alexandra.

"I see," came the reply. "And what manner of illness is it?"

Annabelle thought quickly.

"'Tis one which has the power to ravage one's complexion."

It was the right choice. A look of concern crossed Alexandra's face.

"Then see that they stay right away from me!"

"Aye, m'lady." Annabelle disappeared back into the kitchen, but not before Alexandra called out to her.

"And see that my bonbons are in my room for the evening."

Annabelle bowed and closed the door.

"And so the Yuletide once again," Alexandra said softly to herself as she ate. She directed her gaze over to the great hall with all its magical trappings and sighed. 'Papa' had long since returned to Malta, leaving her alone in what felt increasingly like a strange land. She had no money and the Prince, since their beastly fight upon his return from Spain, seldom visited. No visitors graced her doorstep, no letters relieved her aloneness, and the Prince no longer sent gowns, jewels, and money.

Why? Why? Each day she anxiously examined her face in the small looking glass that sat upon a dressing table in her bedchamber. Lines had appeared on her smooth skin lately, lines she could not erase. Between her brows a furrow or two refused to vanish, creases running from her nose to her mouth appeared to be getting deeper, and her cheeks! The rosy fullness of bright youth was gone and she relied more and more upon rouge not for emphasis of her natural blush but as an artificial recreation of it. Constantly she reassured herself that whatever the Prince's reasons were for not coming round they could not possibly be due to fading beauty, for her beauty had not faded! What was a line here, a patch of dull color there? Pish! Her essential, ravishing beauty would not fade! Ever!

And yet. She fretted about the lines. From her days at court she remembered the purveyors of lotions and creams and powders and rouges used by the ladies there. She had a stock of them all and relentlessly applied them all, screaming in rage when they did not reverse what comes to us all.

In a sudden fit of frustration, she had risen to leave her Yuletide repast and retire upstairs when a flickering light beyond the far window caught her attention. She cocked her head, and ran lightly to the front door – if a fire were about to envelope her estate she would need to call out her servants regardless of their plague. She threw back the door and stepped out.

The light she had seen through the windows of her great hall was coming from atop the ridge that bounded her estate, her Coudenoure. There, silhouetted by the starry night and a great bonfire, she saw figures dancing, children running and playing. Others appeared seated and by listening carefully, she could hear merry laughter trickling down the side of the hill. It rolled to a jolly stop at her feet.

Who were these people? She called out for Annabelle.

"Yes, m'lady?"

"Who are they?" She pointed to the ridge.

Annabelle replied without hesitation.

"Mademoiselle, even though they are ill, they participate in a pagan ritual. Each Christmas evening, they dance to ensure the prosperity of Coudenoure for the coming year. 'Tis a silly thing, but they insist."

Alexandra looked at them, and for a brief moment felt a pang. For no reason, she thought of her mother.

"Make certain they keep away from me till all illness is gone."

She went back inside and mounted the stairs to her bedchamber. Annabelle watched her go. She knew well of all the troubles brought down upon Coudenoure by Alexandra. She knew of her vanity, her shallowness, her narcissistic behaviors, yet she could not help but pity the woman. All she had ever had was beauty, and in the folly of youth she had not understood its fleeting quality. Annabelle shuddered, and went back inside.

Had not both of them retired back into the manor house, they would have been shocked to hear a great cheer arise from the ridge. Each figure there seemed to pause and then rise, moving towards a shadowy silhouette which appeared from behind the signal house. They rushed to it, surrounded it, engulfed it in hugs. It was some time before the cheering subsided.

Ian had returned.

"And where are my good wife's sonnets?" he demanded, pulling Ben and Elizabeth's letter from his pocket.

Elizabeth smiled as Ben hugged their friend.

"We knew that love would bring you home. They are in Oxford, where we have kept them safe."

Chapter Twenty-Three

In the early morning hours, long after the tired trek back down the ridge to the servants' allee of cottages, Ian and Roman sat before the hearth in the cottage assigned to Mary and Rouster: they were, as always, in their room just off the manor's kitchen and had offered the cottage to Ian for his time at Coudenoure. Henrietta sat somewhat away from the fire, listening to the men and dozing in and out of sleep. The others had long since succumbed to the ale and the night.

Boiling water was periodically transferred from a huge pot in the hearth to the kettle that sat on the table between them. Ian stirred the dregs, poured himself another cup, and continued his tale to Roman.

"I fear we have been blind." He spoke matter-of-factly.

Roman waited.

"These last years I have been isolated by my troubles, and by Donoway's remote locale. You here at Coudenoure have always gone your own way. You have been able to do so because there is no easy access to the estate."

"Aye," Roman acknowledged, wondering where Ian was going.

"On the road to Coudenoure from the north I saw much famine, Roman, and much disease."

"These things are always with us," Roman said quietly. "And even here at Coudenoure we hear of the war our good King has declared upon the Spaniards. Such a thing! Fighting for a land we shall never see - one that is not English!"

Ian warmed to the subject.

"I agree, of course. What purpose are good English lads serving by aiding some Dutch city? Breda? Hmm? 'Tis a Dutch city in a Dutch land with its own Dutch army. And yet we are there! Our Parliament decrees funds to be spent on the idiocy!"

He almost spat the words and after a brief pause returned to his previous thoughts.

"No, my friend, I do not speak of poverty and plague such as is always there. I speak of great swaths of land untilled, farms left to rot for the crops could not be sold - there is no money, and a single meal costs more than a poor man might earn in a month."

They drank in silence.

"Children and women beg all along the roads for the value of a pence is naught and they cannot purchase food."

"'Tis the currency, then, that causes the trouble?"

Ian thought for a moment.

"It is de-valued, quite definitely, but Roman, the very air seems to be full of trouble and dread of the future. There is fear that the fog of war may yet descend upon our own land, and for no purpose as can be discerned by the common folk. They say lunacy has gripped the King."

Roman nodded.

"Why does he insist upon war with Spain? God's liver - it is said that their colonies in this new world across the sea provide them with endless monies. England cannot win such a battle."

Ian shook his head.

"And King James was penniless even before his declaration against Spain!"

Roman snorted.

"Where will it end?"

Ian shrugged as he responded.

"I know not. But I have heard words used against King James that in other times would guarantee one a trip to the gallows! And these words are spoken by many and quite openly!"

"And the merchants? The exchanges? Are they viable?"

Ian chuckled.

"That is for you to discover, Roman, for as you know, while I speak of wool and enjoy a hearty discussion on the various types of wool, I have no head for business. No, 'tis only an intellectual pursuit for me, but I tell you, you must needs find out, for if Coudenoure is dependent on wool as a commodity, and if it is in the same gutter as all else in this country, well then, we could find ourselves in a pickle."

"*In a pickle*? What manner of speech is that? Some Northern nonsense?"

They laughed and moved on to other subjects. Despite their circumstances, for the first time since Anne's death, all three - Henrietta, Roman, Ian - finally felt some small lightening of their load.

Chapter Twenty-Four

1625

King James was miffed, sick, tired and cold. Parliament, with its infinite ability to interfere in his God-given rights as a monarch, was once again creating trouble for him. He had sworn never to call that blasphemous body into session, but Charles and Buckingham had insisted. And when the noble nits sat in their august chambers, they granted money for war, war, and more war, but not for him. Impossible!

Even now, months after he had prorogued the session, he could not bring himself to re-convene that which he considered anathema unto himself and God. But he would have to, for his treasury was empty, his coffers filled with nothing but a bit of devalued coin. Bastards. All of them. A knock on the door to his chamber roused him from his dark thoughts. After a moment, Buckingham appeared.

Ah, the Duke of Buckingham, George Villiers. As the young man bowed, James sipped his wine and examined the visage before him with a curious eye. Dressed in impeccably fine blue silk pantaloons and the softest of silk hosiery, Villiers' legs were fashionably slim and muscled. His vest, also of blue silk, was cut with the finest of velvets. James wondered how, even upon the stipend he himself granted his favorite, the man could afford such lavish outfits. He seemed never to wear the same one twice! Sensing James' inspection, Villiers obligingly swirled a slow turn. Aye. A curve of lip indicated the King's approval . . . and pleasure.

How could a man be such, James wondered, watching in mesmerized admiration. Even now, years after he had first met him, Villiers seemed unchanged, untouched, either by time or sorrow or the vagaries of life that had befallen James himself. The King had always been awkward, had seen trouble as a child for his lack of manliness, had been viewed as uncouth upon his arrival from the north. His love of drink and slovenly manner had slowly overtaken him until now, in his prime, he felt himself coming apart. Was it the constant bouts of dysentery which brought him such physical misery? Or perhaps the drink itself that now brought him low? No, it was not those things, for he had turned the issue over in his mind many times before. It was his son, Charles, who was bringing all misfortune to him. He knew this for fact.

When had it all begun, his dislike of his own child – the kingdom's only heir? When had dislike turned to distrust and suspicion and finally, to hate?

With an involuntary shudder, James reviewed the mental list that ran endlessly round his mind. It had come upon him quickly, he believed. One day, his court did his bidding, his courtiers were his own. The next, he heard giggles and rumors from the dark corners of his palaces: the old man was drunk again; the King was aged and should move on, make room for new blood; the King was addled; the King was a holdover from some long-forgotten medieval time.

Talk such as this had led to Parliament giving voice to young Charles' aims of declaring war on Spain - and for what? To defend some Dutch land? What rubbish! And with no money for conscription, no money for a navy or weapons or anything! Nothing at all!! Yet he, James, was forced to go along and Parliament as well. Why? Because the future lay with Charles, not with him. Infuriating!

Villiers again interrupted his dark thoughts, this time by re-filling his wine cup and settling in opposite him.

"And why does His Majesty frown today?" he asked brightly.

"You know damn well why 'His Majesty' frowns today. You desert me, Steenie, you really do."

Villiers leaned back and laughed.

"*Steenie.* I so love it when you call me that. I love it as much as others hate it!"

For the first time that day, James smiled.

"Oh, aye, they do, Steenie, they do, but 'tis their own trouble, not mine, for you are as beautiful as St. Stephen, and if you were not, well, I would not call you thus!"

He thought back to the day many years earlier when he had explained his fascination with Villiers to his Privy Council:

> *"You may be sure that I love Buckingham more than anyone else and more than you who are here assembled. I wish to speak on my own behalf and not have it thought to be a defect. Jesus Christ did the same and therefore I cannot be blamed. Christ had John and I have George."*

Villiers poured himself a drink and laughed. After a moment, James continued.

"My health is not good, you see."

Villiers shook his head.

"No, no! 'Tis fine. Dysentery is a mysterious condition – it will leave you by and by."

"Well, 'tis my son's fault. Charles causes me such pains with his extravagant war."

"Sire, Prince Charles felt that Virginia would provide resources for our war against Spain."

"Virginia! Really, does the place even exist? If it does, it bankrupted The London Company - why, we had to declare it a colony of our realm this year just to assure its continuance! And Charles thought to bet the kingdom on it supporting a war? What folly is that?"

Villiers remained quiet. There came a knock on the door.

"Ah, 'tis the very man of whom we speak." James voice went flat.

A deep bow and Charles strode forward.

"Good day, Majesty."

Stony silence was the only reply.

"Have I interrupted a private conversation?"

"No," with a calculated look and wicked wink at Villiers, ". . . *Steenie* and I were just discussing your foolish war."

Charles refused to rise to the bait.

"Fine, Majesty, fine. I have come to fetch George to go riding. George, you promised you would."

With a shrug and an innocent smile towards James, Villiers rose. A deep bow, and they were gone.

"Bastards." James spoke the words aloud.

More wine.

"All of them. Bastards."

*****

Much later, George and Charles sat beneath a shady elm.

"You must continue to be respectful to your father, Charles. He is King yet."

Charles waved his hand and snorted.

"I did not call you out here away from court to be schooled about my diseased father."

"I did not think you did."

"We have a problem with which we must deal."

"*We*?"

"Yes, George, *we*. 'Tis about that tartlette who seduced me when I was barely a lad."

Villiers roared with laughter.

"My Lord, she was no tart-lette . . ." He lay heavy emphasis on the last syllable, ". . . she was and is a *fully-blown tart*! And besides, she was the devil's own. Very seductive. You stood no chance." He twirled his mustache and smiled, remembering Alexandra's charms.

"I am glad you find it amusing, for I have received a letter from the full-blown tart and she is coming to court!"

George sat up straight. He had not forgotten his midnight ride, his kidnapping of a baron's daughter from her own wedding, his role in denying said baron his own property rights.

"'Tis not our affair, I assure you, Charles. If King James had not believed the maid and her mother to be a coven of unusual power, we would not have been able to prey upon their innocence."

"You are not listening."

Charles' voice was noticeably angry.

"She wrote to say that she hears of King James' many illnesses . . ."

"Half the kingdom knows of King James' illnesses! That means nothing . . ."

"*And,*" Charles ignored the interruption and continued, ". . . she has also heard that I plan to marry upon my ascension to the throne."

Villiers cocked his head, suddenly listening.

"Since she intends to be my bride – *so she writes* – she will come to court and assume her rightful place beside me on the throne."

"'Tis bold on her part, I must say."

"That is it? *'Tis bold'* is your assessment of my situation? Do you not understand the veiled threat she is issuing in her own charming way?"

Charles color and voice rose.

"My prince, her threat is hardly veiled. Does she have knowledge of you which she might share, knowledge that, shall we say, should it be spread abroad, would do harm to your reputation . . . should you choose not to take her as your queen?"

Charles' color rose higher. Villiers coughed discreetly.

"I see," he said quietly. "Women are such strange creatures, are they not? So shy and innocent, so charming and vexing, so alluring, so . . ."

"Right up until the time they laughingly geld you in revenge for God knows what." Charles finished his sentence for him. Villiers noted that the Prince's color did not mix well with his now sad and embarrassed mien.

"Tell me, Alexandra is not still satisfied with the beautiful estate you gave her?"

"Apparently not."

They pondered the situation.

"Prince Charles, she may not return to court – that much is clear. Her father died some years ago so there is no problem there."

"He was not her father, as it turns out."

"*Really*." Charles did not catch the sarcasm underlying Villiers' one word response.

More pondering ensued.

"Tell me," began Charles slowly, "How ill is my father?"

"Quite."

"And was it not him who declared them witches at the time of the abduction? Indeed, that was the reason given for whisking them away."

Villiers caught a hint of Charles' direction.

"Yeeeesss. His own writ declared them so and commanded that they be locked away - at the very least." Villiers declined to mention the author and true signatory of the writ.

"Exactly! The event was none of my doing! And it is only fear of apprehension by my *illustrious* father that keeps the baron and his brood from claiming what is rightfully theirs!"

"King James could, I suppose . . ."

"Yes? *Yes*?"

". . . could issue another writ, revoking the first. If we could be but sure that Alexandra would not come dragging her tired self into court, there would be no trace of the deceit."

"The baron - what was his name again - might see then come to the situation in a different light," Charles thought aloud.

Villiers spoke.

"The baron will not be eager to bring the matter to anyone's attention. His fear of losing his wife and daughter has led to his acquiescence to the lie all these years. No. He will not tempt the fates with his own wrath. And with the King ill, and the crown to pass to you shortly, there is no one who need find out."

"And Alexandra?"

"Ah, the Lady Alexandra is a problem."

"Indeed."

Villiers rose and snapped his fingers.

"I have it! When we turn her out, we must be certain to do so in such a way that ensures she has neither the resources nor the will to pursue the matter further. We must frighten her as we did the baron, strip her as we did him, secure our future as we did before."

"And will you see to it?"

George Villiers dusted off the seat of his pantaloons as he spoke.

"Do I not always, um?"

Chapter Twenty-Five

March 27, 1625

Spring was late this year. No hellebore was seen sprouting in Quinn's meadow; no daffodils pushed their way steadily upwards through winter's frost; the lavender hedge on the far side of the orchard stood as naked as a newborn. The branches of the pear trees showed themselves timidly green, but save for their efforts a lifeless, formless color held sway over Coudenoure. A dreary fog had settled over the estate at midnight the previous evening and refused to move on. It did not swirl, but lay still and quiet upon the land, light as feathers, heavy as the gray seas which wash the ocean floor.

The estate had been slow to turn out that morning. The sun's light had filtered through the sky's gray shroud for some time before candles were lit, one by one, across the cottages and in the manor house itself. The time of year dictated slow responses - winter was not yet gone, spring not yet arrived. The world hung in gentle limbo, forgetting the past, with no present save that of awaiting the future. Soft, still, almost forlorn, almost hopeful.

Deep under her covers, Alexandra stirred, remembering the past few days. Her trunks stood packed - buckled and belted - in the great hall below. The gown she had chosen for the occasion was laid out near the hearth, her corset, chemise, hose and hat nearby. There was nothing left to do but add artificially what nature had taken away. She rose, rang for breakfast and sat happily at the writing desk near the window. Rather than inks, blotters, parchment and quills, however, its surface was cluttered with pomatums for moisturizing, bran water for toner, small bits of soap and fleece balls for cleansing, and various brushes and cloths. Cochineal rouge of various tones sat in neat, tiny pots along the edge. Alexandra ran her hand over her face and neck, while peering anxiously into the looking glass positioned in the center of the desk. She eschewed whitening powders and creams - her beauty lay in her exotic and olive-toned complexion, not in the bleached version of women so popular beyond her native Mediterranean. She was still staring, transfixed by her own image, when Annabelle knocked and entered.

"You know I leave for court today?"

"Yes, mademoiselle."

"My hair requires special care," she said guardedly.

Annabelle nodded as she poured tea for Alexandra.

"Yes, 'tis quite thin lately but we can use a comb to . . ."

Alexandra turned suddenly.

"My hair is *not* thin!" She ran her fingers through a strand. "It is full! Luxuriant!"

She paused for a sip of tea and a jam covered bit of biscuit before continuing to speak through the food.

"And if it is thin, it is because I am forced to make do, here in the wilderness, with the most primitive emollients and washes! Once I am at court, it will be different. Once I am queen . . ."

A sudden and loud thunder beyond the window interrupted her and both women turned abruptly. Up the straight and wide gravel drive rode a small retinue of men dressed in Stuart livery. Alexandra's eyes narrowed.

"Who are they?" Annabelle asked innocently.

"Soldiers." Alexandra paused and cocked her head. "Now why would he send soldiers? To escort me, perhaps, or to . . ."

But Annabelle was gone, racing headlong down the hall, flinging herself two, three stairs at a time to the first floor and screaming into the kitchen. Rouster was near the great hearth, lambasting some child about the timing of his turning of a great spit over the fire. Mary knitted nearby. One look at Annabelle was enough. They ran to her.

"Soldiers! They are here! Papa, will they . . ."

"Annabelle, gather the children and run. Go to the forest beyond the lavender hedge and wait. Run!"

She needed no further encouragement. Mary began ringing the bell that stood outside the back door of the kitchen. It was rung for meals. It was rung for emergencies. Sounds of work ceased: the smithy's hammer paused mid-air; the stable boy dropped his saddle chemise and stepped out beyond the plough horses and mules of the fields; the shepherds called their herd dogs to a halt. With a rapidity which belied the slow start of the morning, the allee filled and Mary ran, breathless, to tell them of the soldiers. Even as her words caught on each gasp for air, the soldiers knocked upon the wide front doors of Coudenoure. In the back of the group of women and men stood Henrietta and Roman. Mary's first words told them all they needed to know.

"Soldiers! The King's men! Here!"

Roman grabbed Henrietta's hand and ran to the stables. There, a horse had been saddled and stood waiting for his customary ride out to the far fields on his morning rounds of the estate. He grabbed its reins and hoisted Henrietta into the saddle.

"But where to, my love?" Henrietta's voice shook with fear. She had never dreamed the King would ever look for her again. What had brought this on? What had she done? Her family ruined, her life taken because of loose words so many years ago. Roman put his hand over hers to steady her thoughts.

"Ride to Elizabeth and Ben. Aye, you must, for we do not know if soldiers will arrive there as well."

Henrietta bent low and kissed him. A long ride into a dark day lay before her.

"And you?"

Roman laughed.

"Oh, I shall be fine, wife. If they should find me, I will die before I let them take me. Now go! Remember, I am with you."

*****

Alexandra pulled her dressing gown tighter about her girth as she made her way down the stairs. Where were her servants? Why did they not answer the door? She was faced with an impossible situation. She had wanted to make a grand entrance, dressed in splendor and utterly bedazzling as she descended the staircase. Instead, she was forced to answer the door herself in a shameful state of dishabille. With all the elegance and attitude that could be thrown upon her ratty dressing gown and tatty knotted hair, she threw open the doors. She did not see Rouster, still and alert, in the recessed shadows of a far wall.

"Oui? Why do you disturb my estate so early? Who are you?"

There were eight of them. Each was dressed smartly in court livery. Their crisp uniforms and the gleaming tack of their mounts stood in sharp contrast to Alexandra's costume. Of the eight men, seven stood slightly back from the door. The leader, the one who had knocked, looked Alexandra up and down in confusion.

"Madame . . ."

"Mademoiselle!!"

"Yes, well, I must consult with my men. One moment."

He turned away and the small troop gathered round him.

"*This*? This is the woman?" He tilted his head discreetly to indicate Alexandra.

A collective semi-surreptitious glance at her went round the circle.

"Sir, it cannot be. This woman is, well, she is not the bewitchingly beautiful creature we were warned about."

"Indeed," spoke their leader quietly. "But 'tis her, for she has the dark complexion and the dark eyes described by Villiers."

"God's liver, man, she also has gray hair, is missing a tooth and weighs more than I. There is nothing of the maid about her."

They stood shuffling their feet, uneasy. Alexandra called out to them from the door.

"My good men, do not fear. You are here to escort me to the court, are you not?"

All eyes turned. Alexandra batted her eyes and struck what had been, years earlier, one of her more successful seductive poses. She smiled coyly. After a moment the men returned to their whispered conversation.

"God in heaven, the old girl - 'tis her."

"Indeed."

"She threatens the Prince? She is a danger to the kingdom? My lord, she is a whore in a dressing gown the lowest tart would not wear!"

"Nevertheless, men, we told Villiers we would rise to the occasion and help our Prince. Do not forget the ill health of good King James - Prince Charles will soon be upon the throne and he will not forget this kindness on our part."

A grudging nod all around. The leader turned once more to face Alexandra. From his hiding place Rouster strained forward to hear his words.

"Alexandra of Malta -"

"Oui . . ."

"Your lease and hold upon this estate is hereby revoked by the King's own word and in the King's own hand."

With a flourish he produced a scroll of parchment from within his vest.

"It is hereby decreed that the estate of Coudenoure shall revert to its rightful and ancient bloodline - the descendants of Thomas de Grey. Henceforward, all rights and ownership of Coudenoure reside in the Baron de Gray, Roman Collins."

Alexandra stood thunderstruck. To deny her the queenship was one thing. To take away her estate was quite another.

"You are mistaken, sir. Repeat yourself."

The man sighed and gave his short speech again.

"You are mistaken. You have been sent to accompany me to court, where I will marry Prince Charles. I am not at my most beautiful, but my trunks are packed and ready. See them here? I shall be a moment dressing . . ."

"No." He had grown tired of the situation.

"You will leave this land now."

With a lightening quick move, Alexandra hurled herself through the doors and onto a nearby steed. No one dared touch her or stand in her way. She paused to catch her breath and tie up her dressing gown once more as she sat atop the horse.

"We shall see about all this! Oui! You misunderstand your role, soldier man. I see I shall have to ride myself to Greenwich to straighten the situation. And be assured . . ." she kicked her mount savagely as she turned the great beast, ". . . Be assured that I will have you roasted upon a flaming roaster of a roasting fire."

As she galloped down the drive, angry Italian words floated back upon the foggy air to the soldiers at the door.

"She stole my horse!" A man from the side of the group spoke. "Rode clean away on it!"

The leader chuckled.

"'Tis a small price to pay to be done with this silly work."

They stood for a moment, uncertain how to proceed. Rouster appeared suddenly at the door, bowing deeply.

"Your Lordship, forgive me, but I overheard your reading of our good King James' decree."

They looked him up and down. Rouster was many things, but none of them fit the description the men were looking for. His round jolly face, reddened from years of hearth-work in Coudenoure's kitchen, his rotund figure with not one but two aprons and a cloth over his shoulder spoke to his position in the household.

"You are the cook, are you not?" The leader asked politely.

Rouster looked down at his attire and smiled.

"Aye, I am that. Would you and your men like a bit of warm food and ale? I have just made biscuits . . ."

The man held up his hand to stop the stampede of men through the doors of Coudenoure.

"We appreciate your hospitality, but we seek the Lord of this manor. He is one . . ." he looked down and read from the scroll, ". . . one Roman Collins, Baron de Grey, owner of Coudenoure."

Rouster continued smiling as though nothing unusual were taking place.

"I believe, sire, he may be on the grounds."

A raised eyebrow was the only rejoinder.

"You see, sire, I believe the Baron may be about, you know, about nearby. If you can wait but a moment . . ."

"We will." came the reply, "I do not believe we have a choice. And if you cannot find the Baron, you must provide answers as to where we might find him."

As Rouster bowed and began backing away, the man snapped his fingers.

"She mentioned her trunks - where are these so that we may relieve you of them?"

Rouster stood aside and pointed at the collection of travel bags that stood in the hall. He then disappeared toward the kitchen at a dignified pace. Once beyond the site of the soldiers, however, he broke into a run. Out the back door and down the allee he flew, almost tearing the door of Roman and Henrietta's small cottage off its hinges as he threw it open. Roman stood by the hearth with a raised musket in his hand. A cluster of similarly armed servants and craftsmen surrounded him. Seeing Rouster he lowered his weapon and nodded for him to speak.

"Roman, you must come, for the most peculiar thing is happening."

Chapter Twenty-Six

Alexandra was in a rage fueled in equal measure by anger and fear. It simply could not be true – why would Charles take her estate from her? He could not marry a landless, nameless peasant from Malta! He needed her to own Coudenoure to assure her legitimacy upon the throne. The throne . . .

She pulled her horse up short. Unless. But surely he meant to marry her. Through the years and the arguments between them, through his lack of attention and his claims that he sought a bride from Spain, from France, from wherever, she had always believed in her heart that she controlled him yet, that she could dictate her will to him as she had done when he was but a gangly youth.

But now . . . what if that had changed? She had never seriously given thought to herself not being first among the amours of Prince Charles. If she were not, what was her future? Her love for Coudenoure was still there, but the place was isolated, far removed from the gaiety and frivolity of the court. She missed those elements of her previous life: the gossip, the banquets, the men. But if she had not Coudenoure . . . she gasped in realization. She would be homeless, penniless, adrift as a beggar on the streets of London.

No, it could not be true. It could not, could not, could not.

Once again, she dug her heels into the sides of her mount and entered the Greenwich Wood. She had ridden here with Charles on many occasions and knew the way to the palace well. In no time, she crossed the high road that ran along the perimeter wall of Greenwich Palace and pulled to a halt before the guardhouse. A young soldier stepped forward in a measured, clipped manner.

"Madame . . ." he began before Alexandra cut him off.

"*Mademoi* . . . oh never mind. I must see Prince Charles at once!"

The solider, no more than a boy, looked over the site before him - an expensive black steed decked out in the King's own livery, ridden by an older woman in a dressing gown flecked with mud and forest debris, her hair streaming gray, black and matted down her back - and decided this was a matter for his superior. With a bow, he stepped into the guardhouse.

Alexandra took a deep breath - yes, *that* was more like it! Finally, someone understood her position and the urgency of her visit to the Palace. She smoothed her hair and sat a little straighter in the saddle. After a moment, an older guard appeared, looked at her, grinned and came forward.

"What's all this, then?" He nodded at the horse and Alexandra. She smiled coquettishly.

"Exactly! I must see the Prince at once!"

The man's eyes narrowed.

"Indeed." He spit to one side before continuing. "And tell me, where did you get that fine horse?"

Alexandra felt a stab of confusion.

"My horse? What does that matter?! Open the gate!"

"Oh, it matters, Madame, for you see, that beast you ride belongs to the King, as does the livery in which it is bedecked. Now, the only way you could have gotten your hands on such a fine animal is if you stole it, so I ask again, how did you come by such a beautiful ride?"

He began reaching for the reins.

Alexandra was quick. She yanked backwards with all her might, causing the horse to rear and the soldier to back away. She turned it and almost in a single bound covered the road and disappeared back into Greenwich Wood.

"What was that?" the young guard asked as the thunder of the hooves slowly faded.

"No idea."

They walked back slowly to the guardhouse.

"Should we report the missing steed?"

"Aye, that we should. Go round to the stables, and tell Marshall – he will know how to handle it."

*****

Much later, Marshall St. John rode past the guardhouse. He called out to the two guards who had earlier spoken with Alexandra.

"So you enter the wood in search of the witch?" they giggled.

Marshall smiled.

"Aye, a witch indeed. Was she alone?"

"That she was."

"Tell me again what she looked like – I must be certain to recognize her should I find her!"

"She was horrible . . ." began the boy soldier. His superior raised his hand to silence him.

"In her younger day, she may have been quite beautiful," he said thoughtfully. Marshall nodded for him to continue.

"She was not of these isles, no indeed. She spoke in a strange voice, and there was nothing of a pale English lady about her. She was dark, with dark eyes and raven hair. Well, raven before the grays set upon her." He laughed.

Marshall joined him.

"Why do you suppose she wore a dressing gown? Eh?"

"We know not, Marshall, but aye, she was a site. And she is riding on old Samuel's mount. We shall have fun with him when he turns up."

The young boy smiled at the thought.

"Take care should she return. Catch her immediately and I will question her anon."

They agreed, and Marshall crossed the road and entered Greenwich Wood. He was under no illusion as to the mystery woman's identity. But why Alexandra would appear at court in a dressing gown on a stolen horse – it was at once funny and concerning. He clicked his mount lightly and rode on through the forest gloom.

As soon as he turned onto the long straight drive of Coudenoure, Marshall's concerns vanished. Whatever event had precipitated Alexandra's ride to Greenwich Palace, it had apparently ended well for Coudenoure. All across the front lawn children screamed and danced. Master Phillip, the old shepherd with no teeth, sat on the front stoop with his lute strumming and singing a gay tune while Rouster twirled Mary about in a breathless jig. Roman stood by on Coudenoure's best steed talking quietly to Ian. Seeing Marshall, he shouted and waved with a grin.

"I am off, young Marshall, to fetch my wife!"

But even as he spoke a slow tolling of church bells floated over the cold, crisp air. On and on, in somber fluted notes they chimed. The music and dancing came to a clumsy halt as all eyes were attracted to the scene just beyond the gate.

From down the long drive appeared a solitary figure on a sway-backed nag. The stranger approached Coudenoure at a slow, plodding gait, giving those near the door a chance to study him. A wide-brimmed, flat, black hat sheltered a bony face with a long, crooked nose, while a black woolen cassock hid an equally skeletal frame. The horse was small, its tack old and cracked. If the man had stretched his toes, he could have touched the ground as he rode. The only bit of color about the sad pair was a flashy blue sash with fringe tied about the man's waist. Altogether, they presented a most ecclesiastical tableau.

"So the good friar has come to pay a visit." Rouster said quietly, watching the approaching man with alarm.

"Indeed." chimed in Roman. "He may go to the devil for all the help and succor he offered during the past few years."

"Roman, you must . . ." began Rouster but Roman cut him off sharply.

"I must nothing. I am done with sniveling. Henrietta is well away – let them do their worst."

Marshall studied the approaching figure.

"Well, if they sent the good father to do their battle, I believe we can take him. What are your thoughts, my friends?"

The man finally reached them, dismounted, and bowed slightly.

Master Phillip tucked his lute under his arm and disappeared through the open doors, taking the children with him.

Roman gave the father a look that could scorch a hole in the sun and waited.

"I am here to see Madame Alexandra."

"Then you may go to hell." Roman smiled so pleasantly as he spat the words out that a full ten seconds passed before their import hit home and a collective gasp went round the group. He continued in the same convivial tone.

"I am Roman Collins. This is my estate. The lady you mention has been turned out by the King's guard so that Coudenoure might be returned to the line of Thomas de Grey, its rightful owners. Now, perhaps you want to rethink the purpose of your visit?" Again, Roman sat with blazing anger barely controlled.

The friar looked about, calculating the situation. Several years earlier, he had been appointed by the local bishop to the village of Greystone, situated near the nexus of Coudenoure's farm road and the high road to London. He did not come from a titled family, nor did his education make him worthy of notice. He had anticipated, therefore, that he would needs must begin low in his career. He did not care, however, for his mantra had always been, 'the lower the beginning the higher the rise'.

But when he had arrived at his parish to begin his career upward, he had been shocked. Low was one thing, but Hades low quite another. His faith was shaken to the core, for the parish proved to be a miserable existence with no revenue, a faithless flock and a chapel with a sieve for a roof. The altar was habitually desecrated by sheep and cows who wandered onto the holy ground as though seeking salvation - frequently during his sermons. More frequently, in fact, than his parishioners.

The years passed, some slowly, some quickly, but all shared one common theme - desperation. Desperation, in fact, had driven him to reach out to Alexandra, hoping she might be brought into the fold. Along with her money.

He had steadfastly ignored the rumors surrounding her estate, rumors which, if true, terrified him completely. It was said that the original owners were of Satan, and that King James had fought a valiant and noble battle to win the land back from the coven which it sheltered. Even now, on occasion, whispers abounded about the strangeness of the place, its magical powers to hold all who entered its grounds enthralled in its beauty. These rumors were potent and frightening, whispered by candlelight and carried on the wind. The fact that Alexandra was Catholic also scared him witless, but faced with ruin and possibly God's rejection - for surely losing his parish was such - he chose the lesser of the evils.

Had he paused, he would have realized that the man of the cloth had somehow been replaced by the man of gritty, persistent need. He had given up on rising amongst the ranks of God's soldiers to a position of influence, a position in which he would have time to contemplate eternal mysteries, the beauty of nature, and the best methods to control his always errant flock (guilt? fear?). He just wanted to fix the roof and save a soul or two, perhaps plant a nice summer garden.

A cough from Ian brought him back to the present, and he decided to believe the man on the horse, more so because the man on the horse had his hand on his sword.

"Well then, my lord, may I say 'welcome back'?"

Roman nodded and relaxed slightly.

"Indeed, I did not come to see Madame Alexandra personally . . ."

"If you say that name once more I shall cut off your feet."

The cleric blinked hard. Twice.

"No need, sire! You and your family have been sorely missed."

"By whom?"

Ah, that was a good question.

"Sire, as surely you know, we seek guidance from the noble among us, those whom God has chosen as blessed and rewarded accordingly."

"Indeed. Run along, and tell those who sent you . . ."

"Sire, no one sent me. I came to tell my noble patrons . . ."

"I am not your patron."

". . . no, of course not. What I meant was . . . I came to share the news – 'tis why the bells are tolling."

He paused and drew himself up. All eyes were upon him.

"The King is dead."

Rouster grinned involuntarily and demanded, "Say that again, please."

The cleric coughed.

"I say, sire, King James is dead! Long live King Charles!"

"Tell me more." Roman leaned closer to the man.

"He died today at Theobalds, his beloved estate."

"How so?"

"Sire, he had an acute attack of dysentery, but had been ill, as I am sure you know, for some time. Indeed, it is whispered that what killed him was the disease of drink, for he was never without his wine and ale."

"And you are sure of this news?" Roman asked.

"Oh aye, sire. Why, not five days ago the bishop sent messengers across the land for prayers to be said on the King's behalf. And then this morning, another came with word that our gracious sovereign, he who bestowed upon our realm light and life, he who cared for us with never a thought for himself, he who . . ."

"Stop blathering, and move on. And remember this, kind cleric . . ."

Roman leaned close and smiled a wicked and deadly smile. His blue eyes gleamed, holding the cleric mesmerized in their beam.

"If you should ever, ever, not warn me and mine of news which might come your way, news which I might desire or need to know, you will not see another dawn. Am I clear?"

A giant gulp caused the man's Adam's apple to wobble in his throat as he nodded.

"But, if you do keep me apprised of whatever . . . *intelligence* . . . might come your way, then I might be inclined to look into your situation."

Again, the man nodded. Seeing that he understood, Roman straightened and shouted for a stable boy who loitered near the corner of the house.

"You! Young John!"

The child ran to Roman.

"See to it that this man gets a new horse from my stable. After that, well, we shall see anon about other gifts."

The cleric almost fainted away with happiness and clopped along behind the child towards the corner of the manor house, turning back frequently to bow obsequiously to Roman. Roman turned to the others.

"Ring the bell, Rouster. Call to all at Coudenoure that we celebrate! We are home."

He turned his mount.

"I go to fetch Henrietta and Elizabeth and Ben."

Chapter Twenty-Seven

March 27, 1625

James looked about the room with disgust. For months, or possibly years - he had lost his sense of time - his courtiers, the very men he had promoted, the chosen ones to whom he had given rank and privilege, the very same had slowly and steadily drifted out of his orbit. Oh, of course, there were moments when they still acknowledged his sovereignty, but these occurred almost as happenstance. It was as if they came and went through his palaces as a matter of course whether he were in residence or not. And should they stumble across him (in his own palace yet!) they would automatically bow and scrape but in surprise, as though they had forgotten him and were startled to know he lived on. Forgotten his very name.

This morning, these men suddenly surrounded him. They pretended to have been there for him all along, smiling at him, reverently speaking his name and asking to kiss his ring of state. But they had not actually pressed flesh to jewel, and James knew why. Only since a tertian ague had settled upon him, one that seemed determined to release him only unto Death, had they even deigned to appear.

He lay under deep covers in his bed, his head on high pillows, his hands crossed on his midsection. All eyes were attentive to his every breath. Since sunrise, when it had suddenly occurred to him that they might be right about his condition, that he might not make it through this latest bout of illness, he had decided to have a bit of fun with the bastards. Occasionally, when a particularly obvious feigning of affection irritated him, he would deliberately hold his breath for a few seconds and flutter his eyelids. Each time, he almost giggled at the effect it had on the room: they, too, stopped breathing; reverently hushed tones gave way to a hustling jostle to be the one nearest his bed; peering, wildly-excited faces came close. But then, just when they thought they had him, he would exhale in their little, disappointed faces. Yes, quite entertaining. But between such moments, he could not control his thoughts as they turned again and again the pages of his life. It was as though he finally decided, albeit late, to put some order to his own narrative.

The King looked out the window and was sad that he would not ride the grounds of Theobalds ever again. He remembered the first time he had seen it. He had been on his first progress from Scotland, newly arrived to claim the throne and unite the two kingdoms. Ah, yes. At the time, the estate was almost new, for Queen Elizabeth's Lord Burghley had built it as his own country estate and his son, Robert, had inherited it. Gables, turrets, glistening glass - all had caught his attention as he had paused on the road to London. It was a fantasy palace, neatly proportioned and with serious thought given to its entirety, not just this section or that. He loved it from the first, and in his mind it came to represent the difference between Scotland and England. When Cecil had offered it to him as a gift, he could not refuse. The fact he had let it be known that he expected it to come to him (it was, after all, his favorite) did not bother him in the least. And he had given the man Hatfield in return.

James' thoughts turned to Hatfield, and even now it irked him that Cecil had been delighted with the exchange, as though the tiny, inconsequential childhood home of Queen Elizabeth meant more to him that the grand estate of Theobalds he gifted to James. He could still see Hatfield in his mind's eye - falling roof, overgrown gardens, no grandeur at all. And yet, it had pleased Cecil immensely, for no better reason that it had been home to the sovereign whom he had served. Elizabeth.

Elizabeth. Aye, he remembered now his correspondence with the virgin queen before his ascension to the English throne, and smiled inwardly at the subterfuge in which they had engaged. Cecil had decried her contact with the Scottish King, the backward man of the backward and clannish land to the north. So they had fooled the little minister by writing in code, assigning courtiers and ministers numbers rather than names.

Yes – it had been quite amusing, state need bent to his suspicious and secretive mind. And purposeful, too, for it had ensured a smooth transition to a united kingdom. So long ago.

Elizabeth had been gone now almost twenty-five years and still, her subjects spoke lovingly of her, in reverent tones: "Oh, I remember when she stared down the Spanish ships, the infidels vaunted armada, and saved us all from the wretched papists" . . . "Dudley, oh aye, she could not marry the love of her life for he murdered his wife. But she would never have done so anyway, for she was married to her people, to our well-being" . . ."There was no famine under Bess, good Queen Bess never took us into war, Queen Bess was frugal and careful of taxation" . . . Queen Bess, Queen Bess, Queen Bess.

What was it about that woman that had inspired such loyalty? James adjusted legs under the covers, flexing his toes and settling in for a bit more such reverie. He was equally mindful of his people and their needs. Why, had he not written an entire book (and well-received it was amongst scholars!) on the dangers of witchcraft, and women in general? He had spent his coffers dry, it was true, but his people expected him to be grand and to undertake grand schemes – they needed such entertainment and an awe-inspiring monarch. He ran a "loose" court, they said. But drink was in his blood, and he had needed it to deal with the priggish English and their stiff and formal protocols.

They had wealth, more than all the clans of Scotland combined. And yet they did not see that all of it - their grand estates and gold-encrusted jewels, their sumptuous clothing and elegant tapestries - all of it flowed from him, their monarch. No, they tussled with him over every penny, begrudged him every pound. In darkened hallways he heard the name Stuart whispered and spit like venom from their mouths.

But for her, they yet poured out warmth and love, as though he, James, were not as brave, as determined, as smart, as good, as . . .

Some bearded face leaned in close to his and he jerked his thoughts back to the present, holding his breath and closing his eyes. Hee hee. Yes, teach the bastards a thing or two on his way out the door, he would. He returned to his own deep thoughts.

Elizabeth was not the only woman on a throne he had had to deal with in his life. No. His mind went further back in time.

Mary Queen of Scots, his own mother. Ah, now there was proof of God's intent that women not be set upon any throne. Ruled by ruthless men and her own capricious heart she had died at the hands of Elizabeth, with his full knowledge and cooperation. He closed his eyes again, not to fool his courtiers but to block the memory of his own actions. To deny your mother sanctuary, to agree to her death in return for the throne . . . even now, a queasy sense of guilt and coming retribution lingered uneasily round his thoughts on the subject. Would she be there? Would she recognize him? What might she say to him – words of kindness or harsh accusations? He sighed.

There was no one left now. No one amongst any of his fawning lackeys knew the Tudors, knew Mary, and could reach out and bring them alive in their minds. It occurred to James that he was the last of the absolute monarchs. Like her father, Elizabeth had kept Parliament in line, had managed to reign as she saw fit with no meddlesome interference from that vile body of men. He had struggled with them for years and he knew Charles did not have the talent for managing such an unruly group. What would happen then?

Charles was far too dependent upon Villiers, and Villiers was far too unpopular with the common man and his fellow nobles. It would lead to trouble. Charles liked his fancy dress, his opulent life style and there was no money left in the treasury. To soothe his wounded vanity he had insisted that his father put England at war with Spain in spite of that fact. And Parliament, well, they were in a black mood and unlikely to continue funding Charles in the manner he desired unless Charles could rule them with an iron fist. And Charles could not – they knew it and James knew it. Did Charles?

Something had happened in the world lately, and he was almost glad to be leaving it. Parliament –

why, nobles and mere commoners demanding power over the monarchy! The new world to the west, where it was said people perceived of themselves as freeborn and not beholden to the throne; microscopes, those strange glass opticals which revealed new tiny worlds never even conceived of by his ancestors; strange ideas generated by mathematicians rather than theologians concerning the movement of the stars - what was happening?

Even the weather of his kingdom seemed to conspire against a successful rule on his part. James could not tell if the winters simply felt colder because of his age, or if the temperature was surely and slowly plummeting each year. How could even a monarch fight nature? Colder winters, shorter summers: the wheat crops had been decimated year after hungry year, food shortages and starvation arrived on an unprecedented scale. Livestock across England was not immune to the changing climate either. In the face of reduced fodder, sheep and cows more easily fell to diseases such as dysentery. Entire regions were prey to the icy reality of the new seasonal norms.

But famine was only the harbinger of a much greater catastrophe. Without wool to exchange abroad for other goods - for coin - the economy barely stumbled along. Inflation was rampant and those who had money chose to save it for another day, when perhaps its value would return.

James did not like these sad thoughts, and with a considerable effort he focused on what he considered the strengths of his reign. Had he not united the three kingdoms under one monarch, his United Kingdom? And what about the successful transition from Tudor to Stuart? That, too, had been a key point in his rule. But no one seemed to notice or care about those things now. They whined about money, food, clothing.

Enough! No more dark thoughts. He twisted his mind until an old tune came to him. The words were gone, but the melody was light and playful. In bits and pieces, he began humming its familiar refrain.

The day wore on and James became fitful. He grew tired of tricking those he was about to leave behind. He looked out the window one last time and closed his eyes. Ah, they would be happy now, for he would not open them again. The humming in his head stopped, and with a whispered prayer to God for mercy, mercy, he was gone.

*****

On Saturday, May 7, 1625, James Charles Stuart I was buried in Westminster Abbey. Contrary to tradition, Charles I attended his father's funeral as chief mourner. For once in his life, James would have been pleased with his son.

Chapter Twenty-Eight

December 1626

"People are asking."

"Let them ask."

"They say there is some scheme afoot."

"There is not."

"Charles –"

"*King* Charles, *Bishop* Laud, *King*. Let us not forget our titles, eh?"

"King Charles, our good King James has been dead . . ."

"I know how long my father has been dead. But thank you all the same for your efforts to educate me in that area."

Laud sighed, poured himself a cup of tea, while the new King pretended to read from a random paper in the stack balanced on his knee. The cleric bent low and for the moment left Charles to his own devices.

Laud was short of stature, and sensitive about it. A round face set off by a graying sharply trimmed beard, deep-set hawkish eyes, a beaked nose - he was nothing if not a reasonable facsimile of a knowing, aged owl, and the court jester never failed to hit the mark with the comparison, swooping and flapping his arms while mimicking Laud's voice and manner. It did not help that the cleric chose gray and black as the colors of his daily, habitual court attire. The gray silken sleeves tended to catch the light like feathers on winged flight, and the breeze frequently caught his flat, over-sized cap, flapping and making it writhe like prey caught in the talons.

On certain days, like this one, he longed for his academic community, the only world in which he felt truly at home. Oh yes, he served kings and he served them well, but it was Oxford, with its clubby atmosphere of like-minded souls - souls which fluttered at the mention of long forgotten manuscripts and esoteric facts - that drew him back to the place time and again. Oxford was the sun unto learned men, always gathering their spirits back to its bosom as the sun gathered its rays at the end of day. He worked for the King. But he lived for his library.

As Charles continued to pretend to read the document in his hand, Laud looked up and studied him intently. He was lean-faced, with curling auburn hair which swirled over his forehead and tumbled down onto his narrow shoulders. A touch of rose blush upon his cheeks indicated youth, as did the lean and supple cut of his figure. There was no meat upon the man's bones.

But there was a set to his jaw that promised trouble, Laud was certain. In the few months since Charles had come to the throne, he had seen it twitch and clench in tightened fury at those who did not obey his commands with appropriate enthusiasm. Even small requests on his part were deemed fit for reflexive obsequiousness befitting an absolute monarch. Fifty years earlier, perhaps, men would have bowed and trembled at such a sign. But now? Absolute monarchy seemed no longer to be in the air. The fact that such a term was even bandied about spoke a dark language of days to come if the King did not hear the tone in which these words were spoken - not one of reverence, but of a deep questioning of the past order and the future world.

Laud had first noticed the new King's inability to brook discussion and dissent during the parliament held over the summer.

As he pondered the situation, Charles glanced up from his reading.

"So they wish me to set a date for my coronation."

Laud nodded.

"Majesty, they are concerned . . ."

"Who is 'they'?"

"Your ministers, your clergy, your nobles – all, sir. The country is fearful of your new queen . . ."

"My queen is sixteen years of age. Surely you jest."

How to help this man who saw everything as a contest of wills and last words?

"King Charles, your new queen is a papist, and your realm is fearful of her effect upon the kingdom. They wish you to be received unto themselves through our God-given religion."

Charles attempted to interrupt again but Laud, for once, held his ground.

"The plague was about London this summer, aye, it is true. But the Christmas season is already almost upon us now. Let us look early into the new year for an auspicious date for your crowning. There are many such holy days which might appeal to you. Candlemas, for example, would signify a day of Christian beginnings, of purifications."

"I will take it under consideration."

"And Parliament, Sire . . ."

Charles rose, closing the door upon the conversation. He walked out of the chamber without another word, leaving Laud to curse under his breath.

"And you have dissolved Parliament, *Majesty* - you young fool - and they are in no hurry to grant you war privileges, let alone money or favors."

*****

While it was true that Charles had attended his father's funeral May 7, it was also true that he had married the French Princess Henrietta Maria the Sunday before James' funeral. The wedding ceremony had been carried out in Paris, with his kinsman Claude de Lorraine standing proxy for Charles. The princess was Catholic, and negotiations had been ongoing for some time. Indeed, they had concluded only shortly before King James' death. To Charles' angst, the beginnings of his marriage - the negotiations and courtship followed by holy vows - were therefore interrupted by his father, the man whose shadow he seemed never to escape. Once again, James loomed over his life.

James had been of mixed mind about his son's impending nuptials to a Catholic French woman, a child of sixteen. In the end, he had reluctantly given his approval. Three days after Henrietta Maria's arrival in England, Charles had presented her in London. But there was no pageantry, for plague had all but closed down the metropolis. And as Maria stepped from her barge to be seen by the people of London, a shower had descended out of nowhere, forcing her back onto the stately craft. James would have seen it as a sign.

Charles had been more than ready for his father's passing. Some said perhaps too ready, and that Buckingham, always more willing to serve than to think, had helped the old man along with a posset which contained much more than curdled milk and wine. And they noted too that Villiers was the one who had insisted on applying a plaster to the King's body as he lay fevered and worn at Theobalds.

These rumors were there always, but Charles could not locate their source, try as he might. They were harmful to his beloved George, but given the hatred that surrounded the man, no one would come forward and stand with him against such perfidious gossip. As would prove to be true in the future, Charles then simply proceeded to ignore all such warnings.

The new King understood that George Villiers' deep unpopularity drove such whispered talk, but as he explained to Bishop Laud, it was Parliament's fault, not his. Their argument upon the matter was circular and frequent.

"Laud, do you not see what they were preparing to do? Hmm?" Charles always began with his same question, as though Laud had never properly contemplated its meaning.

"Majesty," Laud always replied, "It was unwise to dismiss your first Parliament so abruptly."

"There was plague in the city, man!"

"Yes, but your courtiers and men of Parliament know full well that you did not dismiss that body due to plague. Indeed, they had moved the session to Oxford in order that they might continue conducting the business of the land."

At this juncture, Charles usually waved his hand airily to indicate the trivial nature of the matter.

"They did not do my bidding and I dismissed them."

"King Charles, you dissolved the session because they would not provide you adequate monetary support for the war against Spain. But because of their hatred for Villiers, and their suspicion of his motives, they have denied you poundage and tonnage as well. This is a problem, Majesty."

Charles knew Laud to be right. Since medieval times, kings of England had been deemed entitled to the revenue which flowed from tonnage, the tax upon each tun of imported wine, and poundage, the tax on every pound of merchandise imported or exported by England. The money had provided a steady foundation upon which each monarch could build the kingdom's finances. Parliament (during its first session under Charles in the summer of 1625), concerned about war with Spain, unhappy with Villiers' influence, and keenly aware of the empty coffers of the Treasury, had granted Charles only one year of tonnage and poundage, not a lifelong guarantee. Concern over the Catholicism of his new bride had also contributed to their fear of giving the new King free financial rein. For the first time in English history, they deemed it fit to deny the monarch one of his traditional rights.

Having gone so far, they continued with what Charles perceived as gross overreach on their part. There had been talk of curbing the influence of those whom it was felt held far too much sway upon the fledging monarch - George Villiers. On August 12, rather than meet the situation head-on, Charles dissolved the session.

His affairs both domestic and foreign had begun to suffer desperately when word of Parliament's actions crept out across the continent. The autumn was full of worry, and a deep unease spread across the land. Abroad, ministers and kings alike took note: England had eviscerated its new monarch – Charles was seen as caught in a crucible: either he must command his own governing body's respect, or he would not rule well nor long.

As the first year of his reign bumbled its way towards Christmas, Charles chose February 2, 1626, for his date of coronation. As the day approached, the plague released its gnarled hold upon London and Charles began to feel somewhat more optimistic. He had no money, that much was true, but he had a plan, a go-around, to ensure that Parliament gave him the resources that all kings (and queens) of England had always enjoyed. They would deny him no more. Ministers, tailors, bishops, ambassadors, craftsmen, envoys, noblemen: all beat a path to his throne. Charles found his new power intoxicating – all of them bowed to his every wish. He had been born a prince and knew well the obsequious, fleeting nature of alliances and loyalties. But this, this ability to snap his fingers and make it so – heady stuff indeed. His most outrageous demands were no longer met with a cough and a low-voiced, 'Shall we put the matter before the King, Prince?' No. Instantly, as though the room had suddenly ignited, men scurried to and fro to make the demand-du-jour come to fruition in the timeliest fashion.

Charles reasoned that if he, just by existing, could now command such fealty at court, then Parliament would surely acquiesce in the same manner. He thought back to the Parliament of the previous summer and its disastrous ending. By denying him poundage and tonnage, they had reduced him to a beggar with cap in hand, a mere vassal at their mercy. To this day, he could not understand precisely what had happened. What had gone wrong? He was King, God's own hand descended to earth to manage the affairs of England, Ireland and Scotland. Why had they presumed to imagine they had the power to encroach upon his heaven-granted authority?

Charles' conversations with Laud did nothing to assuage his anger on the subject. But time, and Laud's suggestion that the next Parliament be so constituted as to hold a majority who would uphold the King's absolute authority, did. Yes, yes - those men of the summer Parliament, they had been testing him, acting upon the change which seemed to be everywhere and nowhere about the kingdom and the worlds beyond its shores. They needed to be replaced; they needed a firm hand; they needed Charles to demonstrate to them their secondary (almost negligible!) role in his affairs and to guide them like sheep at pasture.

Charles enjoyed the promise of the coming coronation - regalia, parades, sanctity - all would be wrapped and focused round God's chosen man, himself.

Chapter Twenty-Nine

Across the city, in an empty lot behind a run-down tavern on a forgotten road, the homeless of London town frequently gathered on cold winter nights. A fire built of the cooperatively provided twigs, leaves, branches and occasional sawn logs was much warmer and burned longer than any solitary effort on any single person's part. It was here that the woman with the strange accent wove her tale.

"Aye, so you seek revenge for how he used you do you?"

The gray hair which flowed down her back shook violently.

"No, do not you see? He has not forgotten me! That scurrilous, vicious Villiers . . ."

"The Duke of Buckingham? Ye must take care and not spit his name out in such a hateful manner, for he is a powerful man, prone to vengeful actions I hear."

"Exactly!" The old woman exclaimed. "He has turned the King's thoughts against me, denied him access to me - the love of his life and the next queen of this kingdom!"

A low chuckle went round the group.

"The next queen? Of what, I would like to know! Shall we all bow before you? Marion . . ." the man speaking turned to an elderly woman squatting opposite the blaze from him, ". . . bow, ye old wench!"

More laughter. The gray-haired woman tossed her mane with an imperious air.

"You will see, you will see."

A silence settled in as a youth put more logs on the fire, arranging them with care. A pot of thin gruel gave a pop and a burble, signifying the evening meal was almost ready.

"So tell me, queen," the man who had needled her before continued on in the same vein, "What will you do when you are queen of all the land, eh?"

The old woman muttered to herself, thinking over the question. Then she rose and without a word and with no reason danced a light and graceful waltz round the fire. Returning to her seat, she smiled beneficently at them all.

"First, I shall have a warm bath, and those who attend me shall scrub me clean, and soothe me with lavender soaps and rose hip tea."

A hush fell as they begin to listen more closely, each envisioning himself in a tub of hot, clean water, with someone washing them gently with flowered oils and soaps, scents and emollients.

"Afterwards, they shall gently dry my body with clothes warmed by a blazing fire set in an ancient hearth. Then, they shall wrap me in the softest folds of the softest robes imaginable. A cotton wool chemise so clean and fresh it almost glistens, silk your fingers cannot resist touching, slippers of pure mindless comfort and warmth."

Each of them thought of their own feet almost numb with cold and covered in straw wrapped in rags – the closest thing to shoes any of them had.

The woman sighed and closed her eyes.

"After a long and restful sleep, they shall once again wait upon me with cuts of succulent beef and lamb and venison; bread warm from the oven and slathered in fresh butter; a fine wine to complete my repast."

Someone started to speak but she cut them off with a sharp snap of her fingers.

"And then, they shall bring the sweets. Candied figs and apricots, sugared pudding and breads. And a sweet wine with which to enjoy them."

Only the crackle of the fire answered.

"That is what I shall do when I am queen."

"Lovely, dear, but the soup is ready. Shall we wait for it to be served?"

A cackle arose as a line formed before the cauldron.

The woman remained where she was, thinking of her estate, wondering what they would do when she returned. Oh, they would be surprised, she was certain. What should her attitude be? Gracious and giving? Sharp and demanding? What had they done in her absence?

A light hand touched her shoulder.

"Come, woman, for you need nourishment until your dream comes true."

The woman stood.

"Of course, you are right."

"Yes, I am, Madame."

"*Mademoiselle*, if you please."

They joined the queue.

Chapter Thirty

In his short reign thus far, only his father's funeral had proceeded in state with any grandeur and pomp. The virulent outbreak of plague that haunted the last days of James I's rule had continued into his, and so much so that even the summer fairs and markets, so common to London and its surrounds, had been cancelled. His bride's religion was not received well by the kingdom, and there were no majestic celebrations of her marriage into the English monarchy. Even today, his coronation day, Henrietta Maria would not be with him. He would be crowned alone, for she refused an English service and was not offered a Catholic one.

But as Charles progressed to the Abbey, a festive air blew brightly. The plague had cleared now and a new King was to be crowned. Perhaps God's grace would flow once again over England. From Westminster Hall the grand procession enthralled those who watched. In solemn state before the King were eighty Knights of the Bath in their finery, the King's Sergeants at Law and their many councilors, and Parliament's nobles. Two by two they entered the grand nave of the Abbey. Behind them trailed eight earls of the kingdom bearing the royal regalia: the crown, the scepter, the gold cup for communion, the plate upon which it would be offered.

Laud had planned the event well. Even the Duke of Buckingham, with the arrogance which (Laud assured himself) cometh before the fall, even he seemed humbled by the raw, majestic power inherent in England's ancient, storied coronation ceremony. No lord stumbled, the King was sober and regal, and the trumpeters followed their leader. Only one small disturbance marred the proceedings.

As Prince Charles entered the Abbey a break occurred in the bank of spectators who lined the processional way. Laud paused and watched as a sudden scream erupted and a crazed woman with flowers in her gray disheveled mane charged the prince. Before anyone could react, she was at his side. With a bouquet of wilted wildflowers in one hand, she linked her arm through his and turned as though she would join the procession and enter the Abbey with him. Words seemed to pass between the woman and the prince.

"My Lord," came the breathless whisper, "I am come to put your heart at ease. Fear not, I have been here for you all along."

Charles turned and stared at the woman in disbelief.

"Alexandra?" came a whispered horror.

Alexandra smiled coquettishly.

"Oui, my love."

"Leave! You whore!" his words were involuntary, sharp and mean, hissed.

Charles tried to move away to no avail - her arm was an iron hook through his.

Guards were upon them in an instant, but Alexandra had no intention of giving up her moment, her chance to be crowned. In a fury, she kicked and spat at the liveried man who pulled her violently from Charles' side. A huge paw of a hand covered her mouth, smothering her screams before they could be heard. Three more men quietly surrounded her and with minimal disruption carried her away from the procession. Had you not looked for it, you might even have missed the small pause in the stately procession. In a small alleyway nearby, they released their hold upon her.

"Now, love, go about your business, for if you do not, the Tower awaits you."

"You do not understand . . ."

They moved to pick her up but a swift bite to the lead guard's hand gave her momentary leverage. She fled, screaming Italian obscenities as she ran. A mile later, she slowed and sank slowly against the side of a great stone wall.

"Leave, you whore!" She repeated Charles' words to her in a desperate whisper, in a disbelieving voice.

"Leave you whore!" Charles had been earnest in his hissed tone. What could he mean? *How* could he mean what the words declared?

Over and over again, all day and long into the night she sat in a crumpled heap, repeating the words whose import she slowly, reluctantly, came to understand. Passersby took no note of yet another old homeless crone.

"Leave you whore leave you whore leave you . . ."

She did not sleep, but rose in the predawn hours, going she knew not where, dropping her bouquet on the cold cobblestones behind her.

For his part, Charles ignored the interruption of his grand moment in his splendiferous day. With a slight adjustment to the front of his robes, he continued on in somber and measured state. Five steps later he had all but forgotten her name.

In solemn state, he entered the Abbey's nave where the candlelight was a thousand fold that of the sun. The stained glass of the windows broke the light into shards of heavenly brilliance. Before him was the throne, the power, the kingdom.

Charles was dazzled, in awe of the mighty power now vested in him by the peoples of his kingdom. They trusted him and him alone to guide them spiritually, economically, in times of peace, in times of war. His face shone and the Archbishop began the ancient questions.

"Will you grant and keep, and by your oath confirm, to the people of England, the laws and customs granted to them by the kings of England, the laws, customs and franchises granted to the clergy by the glorious King St. Edward, according to the laws of God, the true profession of the Gospel established in this kingdom, and the ancient customs of the realm."

"I grant and promise to keep them."

"Sir, will you keep peace and godly agreement to God, the holy church, the clergy and the people?"

Charles modulated his voice to a deep and hushed tone.

"I will keep it."

Charles rose and was led to the communion table, and afterwards to the throne. The ancient robes of Edward the Confessor were placed upon him, and the crown as well. Laud continued the sacred words:

"Stand and hold fast from henceforth the place to which you have been heir and given unto you by the succession of your forefathers and the will of Almighty God and by the hands of us and all the bishops and servants of God. May you reign forever, with Jesus Christ, the King of Kings, the Lord of Lords."

Charles looked out at the crowd surrounding him, placed his hand on the Bible before him and affirmed his coronation:

"The things which I have here promised I shall perform and keep. So help me God, and the content of this Book."

It was regal, inspiring, profound. Charles was certain it was a harbinger of all that his reign would be: magnificent, memorable, fair, just, peaceable. He glowed with purpose.

Thus began his tragic rule.

Chapter Thirty-One

February 6, 1626

On Friday, February 6, 1626, the fourth day following his coronation - still agog with a hangover from his coronation of goodwill and bliss - Charles convened his second Parliament.

On June 15 - in a rage distinctly lacking in goodwill and bliss - he dismissed it. Parliament, in turn, refused to grant him funds.

"Laud! I say LAUD!!" Charles stomped down the hallway and pounded on the chamber door of his chief minister. On the other side of it, Laud did not look up from the document upon which he was working. Quietly, methodically, he dipped his quill, tapped the nib against the ink well, and continued writing. Another loud bang did nothing to interrupt his concentration. Only when Charles came screaming through the door did William Laud stand and bow humbly.

"Majesty, I did not recognize your voice." He said calmly before repositioning himself behind the desk.

"You did not recognize the voice of your sovereign?"

"Aye, Majesty, I just knew something loud was afoot in the hallway but I chose to ignore it. Had I known it was my King who wished my attention . . ."

"Oh never mind." Exasperation was evident in Charles voice but he was too tired to pursue the matter further. Laud had known full well that it was Charles in the hallway and Charles damn well knew that he knew it - but Laud had, of late, grown tired of responding to the tantrums of a grown man, tantrums brought about by said man's own ill-conceived actions. Usually, he could still rise to the occasion and soothe the King's ruffled feathers or hurt feelings. Occasionally, however, he chose not to, instead finding pleasure by pretending to a false ignorance. Today was one of those days. King Charles had chosen to dismiss Parliament and he had done so against the advice of every councilor who served him. And Laud was firmly in that group.

Charles slammed himself into a chair in front of Laud's desk. Absently, he fingered the fine, thick tapestry which covered it. Laud sensed his mood and sent for tea; he returned to his writing until it arrived. After a long sip, Charles finally spoke.

"So they are gone, and good riddance I say! Let them return to their sleepy villages and backward towns."

Laud remained silent.

"And as for money, well, they shall have to fund me whether they care to or not – am I not King? Eh?"

Laud sighed, took a sip of the hot tea and looked wearily at Charles.

"Majesty, your Parliament would have granted you tonnage and poundage and other revenue as well, but you summarily dismissed it."

"I did nothing that great kings before me have not done."

"Great kings before you did not operate on empty coffers, nor did they spit in the face of those who controlled those fundamental sources of revenue. And all of this . . ."

Charles looked up sharply and slammed his empty cup on the desk.

"Ah, so now we are down to it, are we? Is this about Buckingham?"

Again, Laud looked steadily at Charles a solid moment before responding.

"Majesty, 'tis not the Duke of Buckingham - George Villiers - who is the problem. As they see it, the problem is one of a single courtier having too much control over the King . . ."

Charles exploded.

"George is my oldest friend, and very likely my only one! What would they have me do, cut him off and send him into exile?"

"Villiers has presided over several military disasters of late, Majesty. He is seen as wasting the kingdom's limited funds and additionally, he drives a wedge between the King and his own ministers."

"And so I should allow Parliament, that body of ignorant know-it-alls, to impeach him? It shall not happen!"

"It will not happen now, my King, but neither will an allowance for his Majesty's treasury. Had you allow the impeachment, however, your servants would gladly have consented to monies for your kingdom and for your comfort."

"Well, I did *not*. And it will be some good time before I call them into session again, let me assure you!"

He flounced out. Laud rose, bowed, and as the door slammed behind his sovereign grace, he returned to his writing. After a moment, he lay down his quill and leaned back, lacing his fingers behind his head and sighing.

Charles had changed enormously in the fifteen months since he had been crowned. A penchant for absolutism in government had become a demand; a desire for total control had become an increasingly loud dictate; an unwillingness to bend had turned him oaken. Laud closed his eyes. If Charles had allowed Parliament to cut Buckingham down to size, they, in turn, would have granted him a great many things. Instead, the stalemate of his first year as King would continue for the foreseeable future. The only solution was direct taxation of some sort or another upon his subjects. Perhaps an extended ships tax - not just upon the coastal counties but those inland as well?

Laud was discouraged and thought idly of the great and storied ministers of past reigns. Henry had had his Wolsey, Elizabeth her Burghley. Would he, Laud, meet their measure? Was his man as great as theirs? He gave an involuntary shudder, for if he were not, things would go badly - for all of them. He picked up his quill and went back to his previous task.

*****

After leaving Laud's chambers, Charles returned to his private quarters in Westminster. His mood was equal parts fury and fear – never before had a monarch been treated thus by mere commoners! He wanted to chew them all into pieces and spit their remains into the Thames. He remembered his father's warnings: take care with Parliament; tread lightly with the House of Commons for they rise in these times; do not forget that you are the monarch and they the subjects. The last two were diametrically opposed, for how could he tread lightly with such a group of rabble-rousers while still maintaining his position as an absolute monarch, one who was above the fray engendered by such a lowly body? Was this power? Rule? Autonomy?

With no warning, the door opened and Villiers entered. His entry was not followed by a bow nor was it tentative or reserved. It was just this familiarity that roused concern in Parliament. Were decisions being made by Charles or by his constant, charming lieutenant? They were fairly certain they knew the answer.

"Well, they will not impeach you, George, for I have dismissed them."

"So I have heard, Majesty."

Villiers went on to announce his purpose.

"I have information which I believe will please you."

"Then speak it, man, for lately I receive nothing but tired warnings and ugly demands from my ministers and my Parliament."

Villiers leaned against the edge of a nearby desk and crossed one foot over the other. His new shoes - the finest calfskin available and from Italy no less - were shone to advantage by the pose. After a moment of admiration of his feet and shoes he turned to Charles.

"The Duke of Mantua looks to sell."

Charles had been slouched in a chair near the window. He sat up and cocked his head to one side.

"Do not play with me, my friend, for I am in no mood."

Villiers waved his hand to soothe and hush his King.

"No, what I say is true. *And . . .*"

He gave a half-smile half-smirk to Charles as he reached within his vest.

"What have you there?"

"My courier arrived this morning with this list of artworks with which the good duke must part."

Charles snapped his fingers and held out his hand excitedly. Two failed parliaments had taught him a great many lessons, but fiscal responsibility was not among them. And Charles loved art. As the disappointments of rule piled up and as his ministers caught the trouble which the air breathed round him, becoming ever more emboldened to speak against his wishes, Charles increasingly turned to the quiet eternal beauty of paintings. They did not change from one day to the next, nor did they talk back or question him. They remained in their place, silent, never-changing, beautiful, his. He could not find money for warships or to pay his troops, he refused to support his courtiers, but art? Somehow his barren treasury managed to pay for Titians, Raphaels, and more. Many of his palaces were poorly maintained - Hampton Court was a disgrace - but van Dycks and tapestries graced its storied walls. When Laud lamented his obsession and suggested he focus on more meaningful pursuits (such as the welfare of his kingdom), he redoubled his efforts, even when it meant issuing royal promises for payment unlikely to be forthcoming in his lifetime. The Duke of Mantua's collection would be the latest in a series of such acquisitions. Yes, he would purchase it and any others he might desire. Laud would simply have to hang fire.

"'Tis terrible about the Duke's problems, is it not?" he giggled to George. "But at least some good may come of his troubles."

George poured a cup of ale and watched while Charles continued to review the list. After a moment, the King sighed, put the paper aside and looked out the window.

"If only Cotton would come round." The pout and frustration in his voice was almost palpable.

"*Cotton*?" Villiers laughed. "Joseph Cotton? Surely you jest, Majesty."

Charles looked back at him and was forced into a grin as his friend lay out the case against such an event ever transpiring.

"Sir Joseph Cotton owns many beautiful things, and he does on occasion grace others with them as gifts. But my dear King Charles, if you think Sir Joseph will ever, ever render unto you the Lindisfarne Gospel you are mistaken. In case it has slipped your memory, Sire, you were disrespectful of him - very publicly - at your coronation. I am reasonably certain the man would sooner see you in hell than give up even a small piece of his collection to grace your own. Your mule shall speak, Sire, before that magnificent and holy relic is in your hands. There is nothing to be done about it."

He paused for a drink.

"But I desire it."

Villiers laughed and drained his cup as he rose to leave.

"Shall I send a response to the good Duke?"

"Aye," Charles sighed, "We will take it all."

He paused.

"And George, see what other masterpieces have come available on the continent of late. I have heard much of a Titian from Barberini's collection - I believe he may be willing to part with it."

"Not if you do not call him by his chosen name - Pope Urban."

Charles ignored the correction.

As when he entered, George did not bow but exited without ceremony. Charles called out to him one last time.

"And see to it that Laud does not catch wind of my new acquisitions."

Villiers nodded consent as he pulled the door behind him.

Charles smiled to himself. Laud would be greatly vexed - likely wrathful - at his new purchases. There would be great theatre and drama when he discovered them! He would have to make certain that George was present to enjoy it with him when the old man found out.

But George would not be present on that day. Instead, when the Italian duke, with tears and remonstrance's before God in the familial chapel on his estate, finally let go of his art treasures, it was well into 1628. August, in fact. And on the 23rd of that month, having slept fitfully in a bedchamber above the Greyhound Public House in Portsmouth, George Villiers dressed himself with his usual aplomb and descended the rickety stairs of the old place, intent on denying its owner payment.

"If he cannot provide me, the Duke of Buckingham, a decent night's dreams, then I have no choice but to deny him payment. Indeed - t'will do the bastard justice."

George was not the only gentleman in Portsmouth that morning intent on justice. In the crowd which filled the alehouse was one John Felton.

In the years since the imbroglio involving Henrietta and Elizabeth, John had stayed on with Villiers despite the raw and humiliating treatment he had received at his hands. He had not done so out of misplaced fealty or loyalty but for a far more expedient reason: he had nowhere else to go. His family estate had been lost through reckless business ventures past, and Felton's only chance of saving himself and his family crest lay through Villiers.

With a patience he had not known he possessed, he accompanied his liege time after time into catastrophic battle. His liege, it turned out (as all of England was awakening to), had the military astuteness of a fence post. Yet John stayed on, repeatedly seeking opportunities for advancement. But each time, Villiers merely laughed, passing over him for this underling or that moneyed courtier. Finally, however, Villiers had trespassed a step too far. After their rout in Cadiz, he even denied Felton his pay.

Much later, Felton's sister and brother commented upon the fact that for the eight months leading up to the events at the Greyhound, Felton had stayed in a boarding house rather than with family in London. They noted his deep melancholy, and inability to shake free from the night terrors of battles fought long ago. He saw darkness across the land and he attributed it to one person and one person only.

As George Villiers strode across the pub's main public room day in all his glory that August, John Feltner reached deep within his vest and fingered the stiletto he had placed there, waiting for his chance. Villiers saw him too late. With a swiftness which belied his much befuddled thoughts, Feltner stabbed his foe directly in the chest.

"Villain, you villain!" he screeched at his assassin hovering over him.

Feltner smiled. Perhaps he was a villain. But regardless of what might be yet to come, he could die now with the clean conscience of a satisfied man. He crossed his chest, and gave himself over to the hands which clutched at him from every side.

Charles alone grieved the passing of George Villiers.

Chapter Thirty-Two

1637

Elizabeth rolled half way over in bed and caught the first rays of dawn slicing between the heavy shutters. Ben snored peacefully beside her. She smiled and slid from beneath the covers. Early morning, the night gliding away on a soft cloud of nothing, the light sliding into the vacuum left behind. She loved the immutable, untouchable peace of it all.

It would be a busy day for her. She tiptoed down the hallway past the sleeping youth set as a night watchman upon the candles, and made her way down the stairs to the kitchen. Only Rouster was about; all the others still slept. They smiled in secret, silent alliance at their early morning habits. She took a teapot and cup in one hand, put a biscuit between her teeth with the other, and slid away down the long hall to the workshop at the back of the house. Feeling her way to a table, she set her breakfast upon it and picked up a half-charred twig from the fireplace to light the candles. Finally, as the sun rose further, she settled in. Idly, she sorted hairpins from a pile she kept in a nearby cup and fixed her hair up and out of the way.

What was this place that she loved so much? How had she come to it? She looked about. Her earliest memories were of herself, Ben and Thomas working on childhood concoctions and brews here. Here were the ancient pots given them by Cook, still lined up on one side of the great hearth. She began to wander about the room. Here were the notes from Dee and Quinn, amending this formula of theirs or that one. A far table held faded insect specimens pinned precisely to linen sheets by thin pieces of wood. Below each was a wealth of data in some long ago scribbled hand: the name of the creature, the date it was collected, what plant it had fed upon, the earliest sighting of it each year. On another table were reams of papers and books describing the habits and ways of individual species, including those from faraway places in the new world that had found their way hither.

She returned to her seat, knowing that her childhood and youth at Coudenoure had been different, very different indeed, from that of most other girls and women of her day. It had been demanded that she learn to read and write, and when her interest in the natural world began to consume her time and energy, she had been allowed the freedom to follow it wherever it led. Her utter lack of interest in womanly arts had been noted but ignored.

When Ben and she had fled to Oxford, seeking a safe haven from the evils that befell them, she had learned the harsh lessons of what it meant to be female beyond Coudenoure. Her time there had been hemmed in all sides by her gender. Yes, she could visit the great libraries and study their great manuscripts, but only after Ben had vouchsafed for her numerous times. Even then, she had to put up with the skeptical looks and whispered comments from those around her: "'Tis unnatural", they murmured; "What is she playing at?", they asked darkly; "Pity the man married to such a creature!", they snickered.

She longed for the intellectual freedom she had known her entire life, and envied Ben his ability to move freely and discuss at ease with those about them. Only when they were at home - when they invited close friends to tea or for an evening of cards - only then was she free to express herself as one among equals. Elizabeth had not realized the full psychological effect of such fettering until she was free from it back at Coudenoure.

Only time had unlocked those chains, truly, and she vowed to herself and to Ben that their daughters would not be bound by such stilted norms. She took care not to dwell upon the wasted time too much or too often. On this particular morning, she forced herself to shake the mood, spanked the crumbs from her hands and read her notes from the previous day.

Elizabeth worked now, as she had for years now since their return to the estate, with colors and dyes. She had learned which oils best took the deep and passionate purple of the iris petal, and which held it longest. Madder root rendered in fat and oil produced brilliant and deep reds, while chochineal insects, when ground properly, produced a lighter shade. Turmeric root, sent for from the far away land of Shah Jahan, when mixed with fine olive oil from the far south, brought forth a resilient mustard yellow. She had learned that ground walnut shells produce beautiful browns and shades of autumn but the dye thus obtained was far from stable - a few years after dyeing, the wool inevitably began a slow and steady deterioration from the effects of the dye.

Her father's obsession with sheep and wool had provided a perfect laboratory for her experimentation. Even as Roman mixed his breeds, she had carefully measured the lanolin content of the fleece gathered from them. Each spring, when the shearing sheds were set up and the sheep herded haphazardly into holding pens, Elizabeth would have a boiling cauldron set up in the yard of Coudenoure. A bit of salt would be added and then Elizabeth would put a child on watch. Eventually, the wool would be removed and the excess water boiled away. All that remained would be lanolin. This Elizabeth then measured carefully; for the amount of oil in wool fiber had a profound effect upon its ability to absorb color.

This was her passion, her art. As she began measuring and preparing to grind lilac seeds this morning, the door behind her creaked open and Ben entered with another pot of tea.

Ben St. John was what he had always been. His deep-set eyes still lit up at the sight of a new manuscript and he still saved his pennies for the purchase of this obscure tract or that, this ancient papyrus, that new book by some emerging scholar. It was said at Oxford that he was the only man alive more comfortable in ancient Greek and Latin than his native tongue. Early on, his hair had thinned and then disappeared altogether. A definite hunch about his shoulders produced a hooded, closed look. A pair of spectacles, specially made in London for him by The Worshipful Spectacle Company, were always on his person, somewhere. Wearing them required great skill and a deft tilting of the head to keep them aright and balanced. Though he only wore the glasses for reading, the tilt of the head became habitual and those who did not know him assumed a fanciful eccentricity on his part. While his physical attitudes were not eccentric, his clothes may have crossed that boundary.

Those on the estate believed his attire to be the result of two facts: Elizabeth did not sew, and Ben did not care. Whilst they were always clean, tidy seemed beyond their reach. Ben's vest frequently reflected his inability to match a buttonhole to its corresponding button. His shirt was wrinkled as were his pants – the result of having been dropped where he took them off. Most notable of all, however, were the colors of his attire.

Elizabeth moved through phases with her research, and regardless of the color or weave, she demanded that the cloth be woven and tailored - worn - so that the attributes of each dye could be observed over the lifetime of the fabric. No one save Ben stepped forward to assist her in this aspect of her experimentation. As a result, on occasion, he was, well, quite colorful. This was particularly true when the dyes had not been properly cured or were not suitable for wear. When they ran, Ben became a walking rainbow.

Along with his glasses, tucked about his person always, was a notebook or two and a small bottle of capped ink and an equally small quill. When something important crossed his mind, he pulled them out willy-nilly and commenced scribbling. In Greek and about Greek.

In the years since their return to Coudenoure, he had devoted himself to unlocking the mysteries of the origins of the Greek alphabet. His initial effort was a comparison of certain Hebrew letter formations with those of an early Phoenician script. Ben's nightly snoring was frequently interrupted by himself having arguments with himself about such weighty matters.

This morning he kissed Elizabeth absent-mindedly and poured the tea.

"Dear, did the children remember to close the glass house doors last night? Remember - they were playing in there? The muscadine grapes will not tolerate cold."

Ben patted his wife reassuringly.

"Aye, I checked myself. Where did you get that vine, um?"

"One of the barges that stops by the dock."

"Eh?" Ben asked, uncertain of her meaning.

"The children frequently stand on the dock, dear, and wait for barges with their wares as they pass from Woolwich to London. They buy and trade for all manner of things."

"Ah," Ben exclaimed. "The little yellow monkey."

"Exactly." Elizabeth poured herself another cup. "And the iguanas, the tulips, that awful snake with the rattle on its tail that Rouster killed because it ate the little yellow monkey." She paused for a sip. "And then there is that strange plant that devours insects."

They drank in silence.

"What will you be about today?" Elizabeth asked finally.

Ben perked up.

"Well, as you know, John Beddow is coming from Oxford. He believes he may have a lead on that verb in the 122nd line. Possibly related to some Homeric form. Imagine! *Very* exciting!"

"Indeed!"

They kissed and went about their separate work.

Chapter Thirty-Three

Gabriella and Colleen St. John could not have been more different. It was, in fact, difficult for most to believe them related at all. Colleen was square-jawed with flaming red hair and deep, ocean-gray eyes. Tall and lithe, quiet and considerate, she moved with an innate elegance about Coudenoure. On sunny days she could be found near the library window working on intricate weavings or embroideries. Her yarns and threads were provided by her mother, and she strove to let her work reflect their saturated, passionate color. Early on, she had chafed at small-scale works and eventually had the estate carpenter build her a wide and deep loom. She studied the knotting techniques on the ancient rugs scattered about the manor house, she flipped the Flemish tapestries on the walls onto their reverses so that the pattern of their weave would be revealed. Then, with the patience of eons, she learned to reproduce the techniques.

Colleen was not just detailed about her weaving and sewing, however. Her mathematical skills had been apparent from an early age. While the other children on the estate had struggled with their ciphering, Colleen flung out multiplication tables and geometric solutions with the ease of trees loosing leaves in the autumn. Practical problems were her specialty. She took great delight in calculating wool revenue relative to weight, food costs per season, grain production yields and other fiduciary matters for which no one else on the estate was particularly well-suited.

Roman had early on recognized her gifts and promptly turned over Coudenoure's accounts - such as they were - to his daughter. Over time, she had brought order and a sense of business to what had been a catch-as-catch-can affair. Had it been anyone's concern, they would have been pleased to know that the estate routinely turned considerable profit from its wool, its granary and its cloth.

But even as Colleen was the moon - steady and calm in its orbit - her sister Gabriella was the sun.

No one was quite certain of Gabriella, ever. Her skin was soft and olive, her wide, huge eyes ebony with deep black curling lashes. Her ink-black hair tangled down her back in massively soft tumbles. She was tall, like Colleen, but voluptuous by nature. Her fingers were long and tapered, alive with sensitivity. Her lips were deep and luscious, her teeth white, her nose perfect. Thus was Gabriella physically. No one was quite certain what long ago strain in the family's history her exotic looks revealed. There was a story still heard in occasional rumors of one Michelangelo and a daughter of Coudenoure having been his mistress. But even that legend was fading, and most assumed that her dark beauty came from Ben's unknown family.

In a different world, perhaps, she would have been sent to court, seduced many, married early and upwards and produced stunning offspring. But nowhere was Coudenoure's separateness from the world more evident than in how it raised its children. That included Gabriella. But as the years had unfurled Coudenoure's isolation had begun to bleed a bit around the edges, exposing those who lived and worked within its tender grasp more and more to the world beyond.

For Elizabeth it had begun with Oxford. Even in such a secluded and scholarly world, Elizabeth could not help but feel the change keenly. She would manage, for that was who she was. But her girls? Gabriella?

With a mother's intuition, she had understood very early that Colleen would tread water regardless of circumstance. She was enough of the world and her talents were satisfactorily female. She might be better educated than most women, but her character and her pursuits fell within the range of what was accepted as the norm for her kind. Yes, no worries there.

But a Gabriella could not live in such a world. A Gabriella needed a Coudenoure as a sky needed its blue, a mountain its peak. Many a whispered conversation between Ben and Elizabeth had concerned the girl's nature. To ignore the fact that she was different was to deny God his divinity.

Gabriella did not dabble in the arts haphazardly. She did not fuss about with paints and canvases for mere amusement, nor did she wield a mallet and chisel to no purpose. What she saw as she sat for hours in Quinn's meadow barely moving was anyone's guess, as was the message whispered to her by the wind about light and color and shape and movement and depth and even eternity. Most of all, listening to what it told her of beauty.

Gabriella was an artist by natural talent and temperament. She did not strain to see form and beauty – it was her view. Her only view. To think that such a creature might survive in a world in which she could not create and must conform was laughable. Should she be so unfortunate as to be so misplaced, some tiny flame of the universe's spirit would be snuffed and gone forever, leaving the world with one less testament of its profound, somber and mysterious nature. Such was Gabriella.

Ben and Elizabeth had had to remind themselves of this on numerous occasions, taking comfort where they could, seeking pride in their artistic offspring when the only alternative was pure panic.

"Have you seen your sister?" Was how an episode might begin. "Where is Gabriella?" was another. Lately, however, those had fallen away, for it was now well established that if you had not seen the girl in some time, trouble was likely coming. "God in heaven, what now?" and "St. Peter and all the saints, ring the alarm bells," were now far more usual cries.

The first time Gabriella had disappeared she was found chiseling a boulder set in the far side of the great ridge.

There was a minor scandal when, having been missing for a week, she reappeared with two paintings by van Dyck. One, a small canvas with a pleasing pastoral note; the other, a rather large portrait featuring a nude woman stretched upon a divan who looked suspiciously like Gabriella.

Periodically, marble slabs would be unloaded on the grounds by bargemen or by men driving teams of sweat slathered and yoked oxen. While Gabriella ran her long fingers over the huge pieces with a lover's fine touch, Colleen argued, dickered and finally paid for her sister's necessities. Each time such a piece was delivered, Gabriella spent weeks, sometimes months, examining it from every angle whilst sketching unknown figures upon endless scraps of paper. When she was finally satisfied, the stone was moved to the old workshop behind Coudenoure. No one was allowed in until, a year, two years or three had passed and behold, from the stone had come a living delicate figure. No one knew how she accomplished such a transformation

– she had received no training. But the ethereal beauty of each piece spoke to a craftsmanship beyond measure.

At the end of such a process, or perhaps upon the completion of a painting, Gabriella would inevitably fall into a deep depression. She would stay in bed for days on end, or walk the estate without apparent purpose. At such times, her despair became everyone else' despair; for when Gabriella was not engaged creatively a pale and foul misery seemed to engulf the entire estate.

"Oh, aye, she has finished. Have you seen it? 'Tis from God himself."

"Ah, the poor girl is exhausted like a woman after labor. She must rest."

"We must see to her."

"We must look after her."

Small bouquets were left outside her bedchamber door. Tidbits of her favorite foods were sent along especial to her room. Notes of love appeared on her mantel.

Gabriella, like the sun in its sky, was considered a profoundly mysterious and primeval force. She was deeply, deeply beloved and protected by all who knew her. And only when she returned from one of her hated visits to Hades did Coudenoure right itself and roll on again . . . until the next time.

Chapter Thirty-Four

Henrietta stirred beneath the covers. The light came early these days. Years earlier, Roman and she had begun a series of small marks on the sides of their bedchamber window. They had begun as a game, a friendly contest between the two of them. Over time, they had come to love the ritual and its history. She rose and pulled her woolen nightdress close about her. An old shawl lay across the foot of the bed and she grabbed it before padding over to the window. She sat sleepily in a chair and pulled the worn shawl round her shoulders. Embers still burned in the hearth but the scullery maid had not yet lit the morning fire and the room was cold. As she sat and waited a warm voice from the bed made her smile.

"Aye, now, is today the vernal equinox?"

She turned and smiled at Roman. He had propped himself up on one elbow and gazed at her lovingly.

"I believe so. We will know shortly . . . no wait, here it is!"

They both looked at the ray of light which suddenly pierced the glass and beamed a thin line onto one side of the window well. On that side there were three lines, two short ones on either side of a longer one. The light fell just shy of the lower short one.

"No, not today. I believe it may be tomorrow - what do you think?"

Roman patted the bed beside him.

"I think you should come back to bed. I might have, um, *plans* for you." He smiled roguishly.

She went to him and pulled the covers round about him.

"Hush, old man." She stroked his hair and kissed his cheek.

"Get some more sleep and I will wake you anon."

A gentle snore signaled that he was out again before she had finished the sentence and Henrietta moved back to the window. It was her favorite time of day. She pulled her chair closer to the glass and watched in anticipation as Coudenoure slowly awoke. The first sign of life was always the same.

In the morning stillness, she heard the great wych elm doors of the house's main entrance creak slowly open, then close. A few seconds later a figure came into view, wrapped in a heavy cloak with its hood pulled far forward. Woolen gloves covered the hands but in one a small bouquet of greenery and flowers could be seen. It was Ian, stooped now, and with a distinctive shuffle to his gait, but he nevertheless made his way to the graveyard near the chapel ruins. There, in a small marble vase he had commissioned especially, he knelt and placed the flowers. Henrietta had seen him thus a thousand mornings, and she knew that for ten thousand more Ian would remember Anne. She placed her hand over her heart and leaned her head against the cold glass of the window. I miss her too, Ian.

After a moment, she watched him rise, cross himself, and shuffle back towards the main house.

By now, smoke was always rising from the chimneys of what had forever been termed old Agnes' home. No one was certain where the name had originated, but it was here that Ian had established his printing business. The thatched-roof house sat on the eastern side of the estate, nestled back against the beginnings of the great ridge. It went unnoticed for the most part. Ian had undertaken an extensive renovation of its interior so that it might suit him both as an office and as a printing shop. It was here that he went each morning after his visit to Anne.

As he crossed the graveled way directly in front of the manor house doors, Henrietta listened carefully and smiled when she heard the low whistle he always gave at that point. A young boy sprang from the shadows of the doorway. His reaction was like clockwork – he ran swiftly around the side of the house. By the time Ian had entered his workplace, disposed of his wraps and settled in before the newly stoked fire, the child would have brought his breakfast from the main kitchen. A small ritual involving the amount of tip Ian would give then ensued. Through the big window which framed Ian's desk, Henrietta watched the negotiations and chuckled under her breath. In the winter, the child always received slightly more for his efforts. In the summer, he would have to perform additional chores to make anything at all. Some of the children thus employed saved their money, but most went directly back to the kitchen, where, for the same amount, they could purchase for themselves and their mates sweet breads and candied fruit as a morning treat.

Ian was aware of Henrietta's early morning oversight of Coudenoure. In his happier moods, he waved gaily to her as he crossed to and fro before her window, occasionally bowing in a silly, frivolous manner and grinning up at her. Other days, like today, there was not even a nod in her direction.

Anne had been murdered at the Yuletide, but strangely, it was not in deep winter when he most missed her. It was now, when the early signs of seasonal change came to Coudenoure. It had been their favorite moment, the boundary between it all. As they walked Quinn's meadow, Anne on her cane and Ian happily beside her, they had daily watched the new growth uncurl itself and stand, little by little, in defiance of winter's remains. They had found simple joy in the first birdcalls, in the daffodil's insistence on being first, in the slow and stately rhythm of the sun's lyrical arc across the newborn blue of the early sky.

When Anne left, so, too, had his ability to connect to such simple happiness. It was as if her passing had extended its dark arm and collected all such sweet meaning within its crook, sweeping and brushing it into the grave even as it closed over her. It left nothing save deep sorrow behind.

He thought back upon the ruse used to fetch him back hither to Coudenoure. He had been resistant to staying at first, certain that he would live out his melancholy days in the desolate ruins of Castle Donoway. Like a windmill caught too long in a gale, the very timbers of his soul had been wrenched almost asunder. But it was not to be. Anne's family had clung to him, pulled him along, pushed him further, chided him, expected from him, demanded more from him. Most of all, they had loved him. He had awakened one day to the realization that while there was not yet joy, nor likely would there ever be again, there could be purpose. Ever so slowly, he had stopped spinning and come to a faithful stop before those things which had always informed his adult life. They were familiar yet, and he began to use them as faithful sign posts around which he could orient himself to his new reality. The fates, however, were not satisfied with his rate of progress, and sent along a minor, serendipitous disaster to assist him.

One morning as Ian walked back to the manor house from Anne's grave, a sudden thundering racket interrupted the stillness. There had been heavy rain during the night, and the thatched roof of old Agnes' cottage had given way. The collapse was followed by a great billow of wet dust and debris. Ian decided to investigate.

He had paid no mind to the building until now, and as he opened the warped and worn door, he felt himself entering a different world. The place was as it had been left by its last occupants, whoever they may have been. Beneath the thick coat of dust was simple furniture from an earlier age. It spoke to him of his childhood in Scotland - spare, Spartan almost. Yet its utilitarian simplicity lent an elegance to the place. There was no clutter, no decorative elements to mar the austere beauty of what had once been someone's special place. High ceilings stretched upwards forever and as he turned a corner into the main room he stopped and gasped.

An ancient fireplace and mantel stood at the far end of the great space. Before it were two chairs each with a moth-eaten shawl folded lovingly over its back. Next to one was an embroidery hoop and a small basket of what had been lace and yarn. Beside the other was water-stained, dusty book. Ian closed his eyes and felt the peace that comes with a happy home. Idly, he picked up the book.

"Arrian", he smiled. "A pity it is ruined."

The spine creaked and the pages crackled under his fingers.

"Where did this come from I wonder?" he asked aloud.

"At the very least it should be rebound." More turning of pages. "In fact, it would make a handsome and useful printed work. Why, printing houses are springing up all over . . ."

He paused and looked up suddenly, his eyes focused on the future.

"Of course, of course!" he exclaimed.

Almost giddy with excitement he raced up the stairs and surveyed the damage done to the second floor by the falling roof.

"'Tis manageable. Indeed." He rubbed his hands together in delight before racing back to the manor house at a dead run. He burst into the great room across from the library and stood in the doorway like one struck by lightning. His breath came hard and fast and a wild look consumed him.

Henrietta, Roman, Ben and Elizabeth were seated round a large table having breakfast. The look on Ian's face brought consternation to theirs. Was Coudenoure in trouble again? Should they ready themselves for action? What else could cause such agitation on Ian's part?

"My friend, old man, settle! Settle!" Roman pulled a chair out but Ian declined with a quick shake of his head, gasping to catch his breath.

Again Roman spoke.

"Man, tell us! What is the news?" The tension in the room was now palpable. Elizabeth and Ben had moved towards the kitchen where they knew Colleen and Gabriella were having scones with the other children of the estate. Their minds raced with plans hatched that very moment to subvert whatever danger was upon them.

Ian, having bent over to catch his breath, straightened up, and a broad smile lit his face.

"We shall have a press!"

Quizzical looks were exchanged by all.

"What?" said Henrietta.

"A press! A book press! In old Agnes' cottage!"

"Are you mad?" Henrietta was not one to mince words. "Did you not see and hear the roof collapse this morning?"

"Indeed, I heard and went there to inspect. I found this," he pulled the faded warped volume from the cottage out of a pocket. "I was thinking that it would be a fine volume to send to London to one of the new printing places."

Finally he sat and drank from Ben's tea cup. The others joined him with looks now ranging from perplexity to pity. The man had either gone round the bend and succumbed to madness or desperately needed more to fill his days. They were not sure which.

Ben spoke next, stroking his chin reflectively.

"Ian, you may be on to something. When last Elizabeth and I were in Oxford, we toured such a place on the College's grounds. Quite fascinating!"

Elizabeth nodded.

"Yes - they were printing a copy of Thucydides. Imagine! Of course, they had very specialized machinery . . ."

"I will use my money from Scotland to purchase all the paraphernalia we need and to refit and repair the cottage. The main floor will serve as the workroom while the second floor will be my own place."

"You know, I could write of my work with sheep and wool!" said Roman.

"Dionysius Periegetes!" chimed in Ben.

"Color! Elizabeth chirped.

"Our family history!" breathed Henrietta.

Ian laughed.

"Imagine - anyone may write as they please and publish it for public consumption! What a day we live in!"

"And we can sell copies abroad in London and other great capitals!"

"Do you think anyone will buy our folderol?" laughed Roman.

Ian clapped his hands and rose as though he meant to start on the project immediately.

"We shall find out!"

*****

Word flew round Coudenoure – a new project! The estate would have a new project! No one knew much about what it entailed or what it meant but even the children sensed a new, vitalizing excitement in the air.

"We shall have a project. We shall have a project."

The words became the chant for their morning's skip rope. They were the call for the afternoon's hide and seek and the evening's scary stories session round the fire pit on the great ridge. Whatever a project was, the children looked forward to it with giddy excitement.

Chapter Thirty-Five

1640

"Ben!"

Ian tapped his foot impatiently on the gravel drive. Just behind him, the groomsman was already mounted on the driver's seat with the reins at the ready.

"Ben!" he called again. He glanced up at the sky reckoning the time. "Hurry - Oxford is a fair distance, friend!"

Elizabeth appeared at the doorway of Coudenoure.

"He says be patient - he is coming."

"We shall have no time for travel if he does not hurry."

Elizabeth laughed.

"This trip is many years in the making. You should enjoy it, Ian, and not become agitated."

Ian's wrinkled, wan face broke into a wry smile. She was right, of course. Being agitated was what had forced the long delay to begin with. He thought back to the day when he had awakened to nausea and headache. His condition had worsened and he was bedridden for months. Full recovery had taken years.

Even as she spoke, Ben appeared, more befuddled than usual. His dress shirt was only half-tucked and his stockings were drooping about his ankles. Over his shoulder was slung an aged leather satchel bulging with papers and quills.

"I do not understand the urgency," he began with a small bit of tone. He was cut off by a loud clatter of hooves upon the drive. They turned to see Friar Dunston fast approaching.

"God's arse," Ian said in frustration.

"No, just William Dunston." Henrietta smiled as she joined them. "Now what would bring him this way at this hour?"

"His rutabagas are blooming? He found a carrot in the onion bin?" giggled Elizabeth.

Henrietta smiled again.

"Yes, his sense of news is a bit . . ."

"Narcissistic? Parochial? Off-kilter?" prodded Ian.

"He occasionally produces tidbits of interest . . ." mumbled Henrietta as the friar galloped to a halt beside them.

"Good day, sir." Ian bowed to the friar and motioned to Ben in the hope that if he could but herd Ben quickly into the carriage a further exchange would be unnecessary. It was not to be.

"Gentlemen, I am glad I caught you, for I have news."

He flung himself from the saddle. Odd, thought Henrietta as she watched him. Others changed and aged over time: little lines became creases, hair thinned and grayed, a stoop inevitably set in. But William Dunston was ever the same as when she first met him. As thin as ever with no paunch about his middle, she was certain he had worn the same clothing, the same hat, for at least a decade. Why, the patch she had herself put upon his left sleeve during his first Yuletide with them was still visible.

At this moment, she cocked her head and waited. She often wondered if Dunston's interpretation of God's holy word was as his definition of news – the critical mixed in along with the mundane, the profound seated cheek to jowl with issues about which one might be allowed to worry less in the overall scheme of things. Yes, she sighed, the man's 'news' was always a bit of an olio at best.

"Oh, aye," Ian said as he put his hand on Ben's back to further assist him up. "You must share it with the others for we . . ."

"No, no, you will want to hear it certainly!"

Without waiting for a reply, the good man strode majestically through the opened front doors of Coudenoure like a judge entering his court. The others had no choice but to follow.

The groomsman stepped down from his seat and pulled an apple from his vest. After all, it was no matter to him what time they left or where they tarried. He settled in to wait.

*****

"So you see, friends, I am afraid we are entering a new phase of our good King Charles' rule."

For once, Dunston had delivered. A small cluster of Coudenoure family stood in alert silence round him in the library. While they slowly made their way to chairs and settled in to consider the news, he heaped a mass of jam upon his third scone, poured himself another cup of ale, and waited, pleased at the reaction his news produced. Indeed, if only his flock were so attentive on Sunday morning; if only *they* showed such concern when he spelled out what was waiting for them on the other side should they not heed his words and do as *he demanded.* He let a small sigh slip his lips before he corrected his thoughts - he obviously meant they should do as *God commanded.*

He continued to enjoy the pause and paid no mind to the scraping sound in the far wall. It corresponded, in fact, to the exact spot where Rouster stood quite still on its opposite side, his ear against the cold stone and a piece of mortar in his hand. Mary was by his side listening along with him. She patted his sleeve.

"So even after all these years the King has not learned? Does he not understand it will tear the kingdom apart?"

"Apparently not!"

They returned to their listening. Roman was speaking.

"Friar Dunston, are you telling us that King Charles, who has not bothered to have a parliament these long eleven years, has now decided to force Scotland to change its religion?"

Dunston held up his hand.

"No, no, just their prayer book. Really, 'Tis a small thing . . ."

"Do not be naïve," Roman spluttered, "You surely know that such an attempt to dictate by royal decree a change in worship will be viewed as the devil's own meddling."

"His animus is directed only at Scotland, Baron, and their refusal to accept his rightful and divine intervention in their order of worship."

"For now . . ." Henrietta whispered to herself. As if in answer, Dunston added a chilling bit of gossip.

"Well, not Scotland, ma'am, but Scots generally. There was a rumor last week that two Scotsmen were arrested in London and held until they acquiesced to our good King's command."

A sharp look of fear shuddered across the faces of his audience. Elizabeth noted the rigidity that suddenly took hold of Ian and placed her hand on his back in a move of comfort.

Dunston remained quiet. He did not feel the King's acts were out of line nor did he view them as omens of some further intrusions yet to come. In fact, sometimes late at night, he was stunned by his own pliable acquiescence in the matter. Most clergy he knew grew more rigid as they grew older. Their beliefs became hardened, calcified, and brittle. But his seemed to have expanded. He dared tell no one that he was quite amenable to several forms of worship. Of course, he drew the line at Catholicism - God's abomination here on earth - but beyond that, he did not mind. The fact that his grand patron, Roman Collins, Baron de Gray, seemed to have no beliefs whatsoever, and the Baron's family floated through this life to the strains of some silent, chaotic yet consistent symphony, well, no, that had nothing to do with his relaxing of his own standards. And the fact that the Baron not only kept his friary in good repair, but also channeled much needed assistance to parish members through him, Dunston (thus giving him at least some nominal power in the pulpit), well, that did not influence him either. Or did it. No, no. No point in questioning. None at all. He turned his mind to the subject at hand. Roman was still railing about the King's inability to read his people.

"What does this mean for Coudenoure?" Henrietta asked quietly.

A gloomy pall of silence fell.

"You know," Dunston said finally, ". . . that his levy of a ship tax is being ignored by many interior counties."

Faces hardened.

"And he is calling for troops. I believe he intends to war, yes, I do believe so. And by royal fiat he has increased the poundage and tonnage due him to provide the wherewithal for it."

"Everything is by royal fiat," Ben spoke with evident exasperation. "There is no parliament."

"Baron, good sir, if I may ask, how does Coudenoure pay such steep export taxes upon its wool?" Dunston could not keep the concern from his voice, for if Coudenoure could not pay its taxes it might mean trouble for his own current peaceful existence.

Unexpectedly, Roman shifted uneasily in his seat. Henrietta watched him, eagle-eyed.

"Well. We pay them well."

Henrietta continued to stare at her husband. Years earlier, she had noticed a change in the daily routine of the estate. At first, it had seemed trivial. Ian and Roman would disappear down the long drive. Together. Thick as molasses in conversation. After several hours, they would return. At the same time, a great activity would come upon the yard and barns behind the estate. Wagons would be filled with bales of wool. Oxen would be hurriedly yoked and the wagons pulled out of sight.

Upon seeing this unfold, Henrietta had remained quiet. A week later, more wagons were loaded and driven to the wool exchange in London. Roman frequently accompanied this train and oversaw the selling of his commodity - the bread and butter of Coudenoure - personally.

Much later, when Colleen assisted him with the estate accounts, only the wool shipped to London seemed accounted for, and only that wool was noted in the export tax sent to the royal coffers. The final act in the play always came, year after year, when a scruffy, red-faced and sun burnt sea captain would make his way up the drive some months later. Roman and Ian would order ale and food and accompany the man into the library. No one else was allowed. After several hours, the man would leave and a great scraping sound of stone upon stone could be heard through the heavy doors. In the third year of the business, she opened the door and strode in.

Ian was busy pressing the underside of the great stone mantel and Roman was on the side. The look on their faces was akin to children caught with their hands in the biscuits.

"So how much did we make this year?"

The two men stood up, mouths agape.

"You know - the wool you are selling to France? The wool upon which Coudenoure is not paying proper export tax?"

A second later, Ian spoke.

"I told you she would find out."

"Yes, well."

Roman grinned broadly at his wife.

"Sit, dearest, and as soon as we have finished depositing our pay in our bank," he motioned to the dark stairway now apparent behind the mantel, ". . . we shall tell you all."

As they cleared the secret passage and closed it behind, they sat with Henrietta.

"Now you know, dearest, that my inter-breeding of various sheep strains has paid off, and France is willing - keen - to pay quite handsomely for it."

"'Tis fine, dear, but why do you deny King Charles his portion?" Henrietta had asked.

Roman's face hardened, and Ian's turned to stone.

"Because the bastard killed my wife," came Ian's simple reply. "I shall deny him everything possible."

"Because the bastard took my estate and threatened my family," Roman stated in turn, "And I shall deny him at every turn."

Henrietta patted his hand and laughed.

"And you thought I would disapprove? Do you not know that I stand with you?"

"Well," Roman looked dubious, ". . . 'tis not something I would want you to have to deny."

Henrietta kissed him.

"Our good King Charles - may he rot in hell. Now, tell me, how much have we made?"

Many hours later, the three emerged from the library, content and deeply satisfied. They were accruing money against any disaster that might ever befall them again, and they were denying it to him who had caused them so much pain in the past.

William Dunston's innocent enquiry was the first time anyone had brought up poundage and tonnage since that time, and Henrietta was relieved that the man seemed uninterested in the sudden hooded glances which passed between her, Ian and Roman.

"So he is calling for troops, is he?" Ben's voice was flat.

Another long silence ensued, until a cough from near the door caught everyone's attention.

"Shall I bring more ale?"

It was Annabelle, who had served them initially and had waited should they want more. She had also wanted to hear the conversation.

As all glanced toward her, William Dunston saw his opportunity. He rose and bowed to her ceremoniously. She ignored him.

He turned to the others.

"Alas, I have no wife or helpmate. What a joy it would be to have a woman who could see to my needs." He looked pointedly back at Annabelle.

Annabelle's eyes narrowed. The friar was not subtle, and she would sooner eat horse dung than contemplate what he was clearly contemplating. She waited.

"Such a one would be an angel." He continued staring with what he obviously believed to be a meaningful stare at Annabelle. "Such a one would be treated fairly in all matters and would have her *own* household to manage. Her *very own*."

He paused with yet more meaning before adding, "Well, her very own *under* my careful guidance and scrutiny, of course."

He bowed again to Annabelle with an inquiring smile, lest she or anyone else in the room miss his meaning. Annabelle's thoughts raced desperately through head like lightning.

First, she bowed.

"Good Friar Dunston, we will all look about Coudenoure for such a woman as you desire. What a fortunate damsel she will be! I know what joy it will bring a maid to be betrothed and finally married, for you see, I myself am betrothed these past two months."

From the same place in the wall as had previously emanated a scraping sound, something hard clattered upon stone. Annabelle noticed that not a single mouth in the room was closed, as if all sung in a silent choir. She would hurry on before any of them could speak, but she was not as fast as Dunston.

"Ah, but can he offer such as I do? My woman will be near her family, and can participate fully in the life of the parish."

Annabelle looked at Ian with an almost frenzied look of desperation.

"He offers much more, kind sir, or why, I myself would consider your offer!"

"More?" Dunston said with dry suspicion. He had clearly pictured the scene unfolding in a far different manner. The woman was not bright, he decided, and clearly just needed to be told. He would have to be a man.

"Maid, Mademoiselle, if we could but speak in private . . ."

Annabelle ignored him. Her breath was coming in shallow gulps and Dunston noted such.

"You seem quite giddy! Let us speak . . ."

Did God really make such a dim creature as stood before her? Her breath was shallow, in that he was correct, but it was shallow in the same way that a mouse stops breathing, frozen, when caught by a cat. She must free herself.

"Yes! My betrothed in Oxford, well, he, he, he . . ." Annabelle was drowning.

Ian took pity on the woman and stepped in to assist.

"He is at Oxford, Friar, and that is why we were in such a hurry before. We are bringing him hither."

"Indeed!" Annabelle squeaked. "I shall take you up on your offer and shall accompany you to Oxford. Forthwith. *Now.*"

Ben perked up and attuned himself, finally, to the conversation.

"Oxford? Yes! Ian, 'tis quite late and Oxford is a fair distance. Come."

"Indeed."

Annabelle ran pell-mell from the room, quickly, grabbed a cloak and hat, and dived for the carriage. Rouster and Mary moved from the wall in hasty bewilderment. Ian and Ben were out the door in a heartbeat. The driver threw his second apple to the side and before the others cleared the front door, the carriage was away down the drive.

The good friar left immediately. He had been foiled and needed to lick his wounds and plot the next act.

"I believe that would qualify as a 'no' on Annabelle's part." Elizabeth spoke to no one in particular as they watched Dunston fade away to the clipped sounds of his horse's gait.

"*Indeed,*" intoned Henrietta.

But Roman was in no mood to enjoy the ham-fisted and mutilated betrothal attempt they had just witnessed. He went quickly inside to where Rouster and Mary stood, still dumbfounded, uncertain whether to be proud of Annabelle's quick wits, or ashamed at how well she lied. They chose the former, for after all, was not the latter more of a talent than a sin?

"Rouster . . ."

"Yes, I have sent my youngest for Marshall with an urgent message."

"We must know, for if King Charles declares a civil war, then there is much to be discussed."

There was nothing further to be done but wait.

Chapter Thirty-Six

The carriage made a sharp turn and they suddenly left the rutted cow trail to Coudenoure for the high road which would take them through London and on to Oxford.

"And that was . . . ?" Ian crossed his legs and picked at a non-existent piece of lint on his vest. The smile on his face matched exactly the almost respectful tone in his voice. Annabelle waved her hand and sighed.

"Oh, do be quiet."

Ian chuckled.

"I shall require extra scones mid-morning for the next, um, three months."

"Whatever." Came her relieved reply. "Now, let us pray for the next poor maid who does not think so quickly upon her feet, whoever she may be."

Ben seemed not to have heard their exchange.

"We must not tarry in Oxford, Ian, for I fear that the good friar's news may be but a foreshadowing of trouble across the kingdom."

Ian nodded, and they rode on in silent consideration of the disturbing news.

*****

Were there more? Was that possible? Ben made frequent trips to Oxford (after all, there were always rare manuscripts which came on the market) but usually he travelled by horseback. He avoided the heart of the city and rode the cart paths and vendor roads which fed the main arteries. Today, however, as a concession to Annabelle, they were traversing the heart of old London. Ben knew these streets well, and for the first time in a very, very long time, he was seeing them again.

He knew what it was to a beggar and understood full well what it meant to live on the streets. But he had seen it all through a child's eyes. Seeking out food with Rouster and Marshall, huddled with them beneath the bridges and round the small fires that always beckoned to those without, to those in need. He closed his eyes, remembering his 'home' – a place beneath a tiny bridge over a long-dry stream; a small fire pit just beside it; a thicket in which he hid blankets and whatnots found on the streets to be sold later. To say it had been a rough sort of life would not do it justice, but somehow the three companions had made an adventure of it. They had been children; they had still possessed a sense of wonder.

Today, as Ian, Annabelle and he rode in privileged separation from the masses, Ben saw it all as an adult. The street smells - smoke and urine and river and damp, fish markets and vegetable markets and sides of meat and bales of wool - all produced the singular smell that was back street London. Those scents could take a soul back to childhood quicker than a whispered breath. Long forgotten scenes and people and places could be summoned from unknown depths by a single whiff, bringing back memories from a childhood deliberately forgotten. He breathed deep and watched London float by to the steady beat of the horses' hooves.

Were there more homeless now? Yes. More sick? More lame crowding the byways begging for whatever tidbit might come their way? Yes. He knew of course of the famines which beset the land. They had not grown better with the passage of Charles' reign. Taxation and graft had caused massive inflation - those who had ere now, now had not thanks to shrinking value. How isolated he was at Coudenoure! His care - obsession - with his work and books and ancient treatises had blinded him to it all.

Ben was not the only one taking in the unfolding scene. Annabelle was wide-eyed as beggars appeared before the carriage windows, asking for whatever she might throw their way. Even as one disappeared another would take his place. Who were they? From whence did they come and how had they arrived at such a pass? She emptied the small pocket purse of her cloak to them and still they came on. Her heart was filled with empathy for them all, for while her father had told her many times of his own childhood she had never seen it firsthand.

"Ma'am, a penny ma'am?"

"Have you bread, ma'am?"

"Pity, ma'am, pity . . ."

The voices cried out again and again, young and aged, for whatever assistance she might be able to render. Her heart broke for them.

"I can clean your carriage, madam."

"Have you food?"

"M'lady, help me for the love of God help me."

"Annabelle . . ."

"Ma'am, for my child, ma'am."

Annabelle jerked involuntarily.

"What? Did you hear that?"

"Someone called your name!" Ian said in puzzlement and concern.

Annabelle beat frantically on the roof of the carriage bringing it to a halt. Before either of her companions could stop her, she leapt from the carriage and fought her way through the crowd.

"Who spoke my name? Who?"

A circle of weary faces cleared round about her, standing far enough away to signal wariness. It was one thing to beg for a living, but to be singled out by the nobility was quite another. They had everything, those in the fancy dress and sumptuous carriages. Even their horses were better cared for than the best amongst them, them the invisible nothings. They had everything, including the power of life and death. All knew that their situation, as terrible as it was, could be worse, and that such a nightmare might begin with attention from the mighty. They stared at Annabelle in fear and in silence.

Again she cried out.

"Who spoke my name?"

From the back of the crowd came a small voice.

"It was I. *I* called your name, Annabelle."

A murmur went through the crowd. Annabelle turned and turned again looking for the voice.

"Who? Who?"

The crowd parted, and the oldest woman Annabelle had ever seen stepped forward. She was thin and sallow, bent and covered in sores. A threadbare blanket was thrown across her shoulders, almost hiding the worn dress which hung in limp and filthy exhaustion about her frame. Her hair was greasy, knotted, long and white. She held a stick to aid her stiff and shuffling gait.

But as she cleared the circle and stepped forward, something within her seemed to respond to the moment. With a visible effort, she straightened before Annabelle. Her head rose in imperious disregard for their stations and Annabelle gasped. The eyes which looked upon her were jet black, an ebony so deep as to cause wonder in one's soul. Even in such an abject and hopeless situation, a fiery spirit shone through them. Instinctively and without warning to herself or those around her, Annabelle bowed.

"Mademoiselle."

"Oui," replied Alexandra.

Before either woman could speak again, Ian was by Annabelle's side.

"Who is this?" Ian asked, whispering guardedly in her ear.

"This is Alexandra, the woman who once owned Coudenoure."

Ian stiffened in anger.

"The woman responsible for my Anne's murder? The woman who brought such misery to the house of de Grey? That woman?" His voice was rising, tumbling towards fury like a bilious and dark cloud in a bright sky.

Alexandra bowed and spoke.

"I did not kill your beloved, sire. Your good King Charles, the bastard from Scotland, did her in."

A gasp went round the crowd. Spectacle was fine. Even appreciated. But when the drama turned to talk of King Charles, and treasonous talk at that, no one wanted any part of it. The circle disappeared, leaving the three of them. Ben stood nearby, watching in disbelief.

"Annabelle, we must leave - Oxford is still some distance."

Annabelle waved her hand.

"Wait for me by the carriage, Ian. I must speak with this woman."

"No, you must not." Ian's face was red and angry now.

"I did not kill your wife. I took advantage of my situation at the time. Would you not have done the same?" Alexandra spoke quietly.

"At some other family's expense?" Ian barely controlled his voice. "At the expense of someone's *life*?"

"I did not see that, sire, at the time. All I could see was a home, a place to call my own. All I wanted was what I saw all about me - pretty clothes, pretty houses, pretty situations. I have paid and paid again for my past."

Ian listened to her in stony anger as she continued.

"Look!" She opened her arms as though displaying herself. "See how I have paid for my desire! Do not wish me ill, monsieur, for it is I who have paid . . . with *my* life."

He opened his mouth to reply, but she would not let him speak.

"Tut, tut. Yes, sire, I have lost my life as well, for I now live in hell - do you not see it?"

Again she opened the blanket which served as a cloak, revealing her skeletal form beneath.

Appalled at the sight, Ian did not respond.

"Ummm," she nodded at him. "Yes. You see. It was I who had to learn, I who fell to reality. Your wife is safe in heaven, there by the hands of King Charles and George Villiers. But I . . . I *live* on, do I not?" A withered, wry smile escaped her lips.

Annabelle felt a swirling sensation in her breast. She clutched Ian by his arm and dragged him back to the carriage.

"We cannot leave her."

"Oh, we can indeed and we will." Ian was wrought. "Ben, tell Annabelle we must go."

Ben looked at Alexandra. She leaned on her stick, eyeing them more with curiosity than hope. Once, a long time ago, he had been her. He had lived on the streets himself and knew what it was to be hungry, exhausted and without a future. What had happened to change all, he wondered to himself?

A chance meeting with Quinn, a random kindness. That was what had happened. And like dominoes on a board, the fates of so many had shifted, for Marshall, Rouster, himself. Everything had changed. Without that one freakish moment, he would still be Alexandra. He turned to Ian.

"Give me money." As he spoke he fished within his own pockets.

"No."

"Ian, do not harden your heart in this way. Life is bitter, I know, but being callous only leads to meanness within one's spirit. That is not who you are."

Ian stared at him in blind confusion. Ben held out his hand. Before he could take the coins proffered, however, Annabelle grabbed them.

"Now give me yours, Ben."

He did as he was told.

"I shall stay and see to the old bird."

"Your father . . ." began Ben.

"My father would be proud," Annabelle said simply.

Ian boarded the carriage cursing loudly.

"Damn King Charles and Villiers and all who took my Anne. Anne! *Anne*!" he screamed. "Damn them all to hell! Damn them all . . ." His words dissolved into deep and eternal sobs.

"What will you do?"

"I do not know."

"How will you travel back to Coudenoure?"

"I will find my way."

"London takes advantage of those who do not know her."

Annabelle looked at Ben.

"We . . ." she nodded to Alexandra, ". . . will be fine. Go to Oxford and I shall see you at Coudenoure anon."

"Sire," interjected Alexandra with quiet dignity, "I shall see to her myself, for I know the city well. She will come back to you as she leaves you."

Ben jumped into the carriage and shouted at the driver before turning one last time to Annabelle.

"Why do you do this?"

"Because I cannot save them all."

The horses jumped then trotted on. Annabelle watched them go, wondering what she was doing.

"And so, the servant becomes the served," said Alexandra. "Shall we find something to eat?"

They moved off together down an alley, the old ragged crone and the young woman from Coudenoure.

Chapter Thirty-Seven

It was one thing to behave nobly, quite another to figure out a workable scheme. Annabelle purchased hot ale and bread from a street stall and they now leaned against a nearby wall. Alexandra dipped her bread in the steaming cup and closed her eyes as she ate.

"Heavenly," she declared as over and over again she sopped her toast. At last, she tilted the cup and drained it greedily. Annabelle watched her with pity and foreboding. What now? What now?

Alexandra read her mind.

"So what to do now, um?"

Annabelle nodded.

"Mademoiselle . . ." she began.

Tears flowed down Alexandra's face.

"My child, how long since anyone catered to my desires? Ah, *mademoiselle* – it meant everything to me. How kind you are to remember. How kind."

She grasped her by the hands and looked intently into her eyes.

"Will you leave me now to face my future? Will you?"

Annabelle shook her head.

"I have a plan, but I am not certain you will like it."

"Does it take me away from all this?" Alexandra waved her hand and Annabelle smiled.

"Oui, mademoiselle, it does indeed."

"Then I am at your mercy and your service, for you save me." Alexandra gave a crooked bow and leaned in to listen closely.

*****

At the inn that night, Ian had retired without pleasantries, and the next morning brought more of the same taciturn behavior. As they rode along and the hours passed, no words were spoken in the carriage. Ian sat stiffly by the far window, gazing out. Ben fussed with his manuscripts, surreptitiously glancing at his companion from time to time, but leaving him be. Nothing could assuage Ian's pain, and it would be ignorant and shallow to think otherwise. They rode on.

What were the odds? Ben could not take his mind away from the sheer coincidence of their encounter with Alexandra. He was not a religious man, but surely it could not be happenstance that she was there at the exact moment they passed by. If there be meaning on a grand scale, then surely there must be some purpose to what had happened. But what was it? He did not worry for Annabelle for he knew her to be capable and level-headed. But as for Alexandra – he shook his head, wondering what was going through Annabelle's mind.

Finally, Ian coughed as though reading his thoughts.

"Do not worry, Ben. I am fine."

"Um." Ben said quietly. "We are coming into Oxford now."

"'Tis fine, 'tis fine," Ian mumbled as he watched the landscape slide by out the narrow carriage window. After a moment's silence, he continued abruptly and decisively.

"I believe, Ben, that I shall not tarry in Oxford."

Ben shot him a quizzical look.

"No, I shall visit the print shop and purchase what I want there, and start back for Coudenoure on the morrow. No need to stay. No need at all."

He ignored the piercing look from Ben and returned to his private thoughts. The sight of Alexandra had shaken him badly. Without warning, he had been thrown back to that night, that time, that place. Enough time had passed that he knew he should forgive all who had taken Anne from him. But he could not. Alexandra claimed that living was worse than Anne's fate but she was wrong. Clever – that woman had always been clever. Was that how she justified her own existence in the face of his beloved's death? As the carriage pulled to a halt on a narrow cobbled way, he cleared his mind. After all, today was the day for which he had long waited.

Jonners Publishers, a small printing concern in Oxford, was closing its doors. Its owner had died in the plague that had swept Oxford the previous summer. His daughter married a Londoner and wanted nothing to do with what had been her father's obsession. She had grown up with ink and print blocks and books and pamphlets and paper hung from rope attached to the print shop walls. She had watched the crabbed and worried authors come and go as her father patiently set their text and pressed it onto page after page. It was not her world, not her passion, and when she learned that a gentleman from an estate in the south - one Coudenoure - was seeking to purchase the tools necessary for publishing, she had contacted Ian immediately. Their correspondence had precipitated his visit today.

Ian walked the narrow cobbled street with purpose, but much of the joy he had felt in the morning had now seeped away, leaving him ragged and sad. He clanged the small bell on the side of the shop front and as the woman and her new husband showed him in, he smiled pleasantly if vacantly. For the next two hours, he and Ben were educated in the book making process. At any other time, Ian would have been passionately attuned to their instruction, but today he could barely evince interest. As they moved to the back of the shop into a binding room, he held up his hand.

"Madame, I am convinced. I would like to purchase the shop in its entirety." His voice was hollow. All he really wanted was to go home.

Her husband stepped forward with a broad smile.

"Well, sir, let us talk!"

Another hour and it was done. They would dismantle everything and send it along to Coudenoure before the next full moon. Ian was out the door and in the carriage before the ink on the contract was dry.

"Ian, shall we go home? Do you wish to visit the booksellers here about - they usually have an interesting selection."

Ian shook his head.

"Let us return to Coudenoure," he said quietly.

"It shall be quite something to set up a press in Agnes' Cottage!"

But Ian could not be cajoled into conversation. After some time, Ben left him to his thoughts once more. Someone had opened the sky and stolen all the joy from his world, he thought. All the joy indeed. He returned to his manuscripts.

Chapter Thirty-Eight

Oliver Cromwell was neither tall nor short, neither commanding nor shrinking in mien. He seemed, at first glance, to be a milk-toast sort of a man. There was nothing about his physical appearance or posture that would lead anyone to guess correctly really anything about him. His hair was thin and thinning, a light brown, bleaching slightly lighter under the sunlight. His eyes were neither blue nor gray, but of a milky cornflower color. He had a prominent, fleshy nose which, along with a rather prominent mole on his lower forehead, gave his narrow face a bit of character. Beyond that, there was nothing remarkable in his countenance or appearance.

Initially then, when he spoke, one might be surprised to note a certain eloquence in his tone and verbiage. After all, it was not what was expected from such an ordinary specimen. He articulated surprisingly deep thoughts for one so mundane in appearance. But should he continue to speak, then one began to get the true measure of the man. His voice was his instrument, rising like thunder in anger, softening to butter when appealing, flowing like a mountain rill over his opponents' arguments and counter-ideas. He was the ideal man for public debate, public position – he could marshal his thoughts in a second and his stentorious voice carried above all others. And as it chanced (in God's well-planned universe, he was certain), he was also a member of Parliament, the very place where his talents might be exercised to their utmost.

Cromwell's horse suddenly shied up, and pulled him from his reverie – an owl had swooped low across their path startling the bay. He returned to his thoughts, reckoning the years since he first began his service to King Charles. He corrected himself grimly: to the kingdom of England.

How long now? The steed and the man plodded on in mute harmony. He had come to London to serve as the representative for Huntingdon in 1628, but Charles had immediately prorogued the assembly, choosing to rule in absolutist fashion since that time.

And now, well, in hindsight the events leading up to the present day had a sense of inevitability about them. A sense of doom, perhaps? No. But a darkening of the landscape? An obscuring of the future? Definitely.

He did not ride alone through the silent wood. A cough from the man who rode the trail before him brought him round and he emerged from the cloak of his thoughts.

The man's shoulders stooped, and Cromwell wondered briefly if he were awake.

"St. John! Marshall!"

Yes, the shoulders straightened and the man shifted in his saddle.

"Aye," came the response thrown over his shoulder.

"So give me the news from Scotland once more."

Marshall sighed but did not speak. Fatigue ate at him from the inside out – it began in the marrow of his bones and did not stop until it blew from the hair on his skin. But Cromwell did not care, as evidenced in his tone.

"Tell me again what you know," he repeated as their steeds picked their way slowly along an overgrown path in Greenwich Wood. He spoke loudly so that Marshall would surely hear.

"I have told you all I know, sir."

"Pray tell it once more, for perhaps there will be some detail you will remember as you do, one perhaps left out earlier."

Marshall sighed. He had ridden hard during the night in order to deliver the news to Cromwell. England was at war. With Scotland of all places.

"The King is angry, and a rabble has collected along the borderlands between England and Scotland."

"Why?"

Again Marshall sighed.

"The King's command reached them, that is why. He demanded that all Scotsmen worship as he deems they should. 'Tis not popular."

"Indeed. Continue."

"As you know, they have refused to heed his command and he, in turn, has decided it must be enforced, through might if necessary."

"If necessary?"

Marshall smiled.

"Our good King Charles did not wait for diplomacy or tactful negotiation. He rode north and engaged the Scottish lords."

"And the battle?"

Marshall laughed tiredly.

"The battle - if you wish to glorify the fracas with that name - was joined near Turriff."

They broke the wood and found themselves in the meadow on the far side of Coudenoure. He waited for Cromwell to pull near before continuing.

"Neither army wanted a fight, and an uneasy peace has been reached. But sir, I believe that this rebellion is but a precursor to civil violence here in our own land."

"Aye, I fear I must agree with you wholeheartedly." Cromwell let his horse graze. He looked at the great ridge which rose on the far side of the field. Marshall continued in a lower voice.

"I have ridden hence to tell you this: King Charles lives in the deep past. He has no concept of modern times and the men of Parliament have no desire - nay, will not - go back to an absolute monarchy. 'Tis a recipe for civil war. You know this already. I have ridden hard to tell you that the events are now upon us."

"You mean 'war' is now upon us."

Marshall shrugged, "You may call it by any name you wish, sir. But 'tis civil conflict and it will not end well for one side or the other. I prefer for it to end well for *mine*."

Cromwell chose his words carefully now.

"And so you insist that today, yes today, I come and meet some isolated noble family . . ."

"I do." Marshall did not back away from his plan. He continued.

"When the war engulfs our land, Baron de Grey will stand with us. I am certain."

"How can you know for sure?"

"That is something you must hear from the Baron himself. Now, let us go on. I am tired and must be back at the Palace before nightfall."

Without waiting for an answer, he urged his horse forward.

Chapter Thirty-Nine

The doors were thrown back upon their hinges. A screaming band of children ran into the house waving stick swords and wearing hand-me-downs in various states of disrepair. They were unified, however, by the red strip of fabric tied round each of their foreheads. Willy-nilly they evaded Mary's attempts to stop them at the great hall and shouted their way into the library. Ben and Ian looked up from the manuscript they were examining.

"Where is King Roman?" demanded the boy who was obviously their leader. He alone wore a yellow kerchief rather than a red strip.

"You will have to make do with Prince Ian," Ian chuckled. "Now, pray tell, what brings King Roman's army to the castle?"

"Enemies!" They all shouted. "Enemies are approaching across the meadow!"

"Be gone," Ben waved at them, "We have work to do." He shouted through the open door towards the kitchen.

"Rouster . . ." No reply. "Rouster - feed these rogue soldiers, would you?"

One of the soldiers squealed out before anyone could answer.

"Look!" The child pointed through the mullioned window that looked out onto Quinn's meadow and the front of Coudenoure. "They are upon us!"

"Man your battle stations!" The leader screamed and the mob disappeared as quickly as it had come.

Ian moved to the window and laughed.

"'Tis Marshall!"

He too disappeared through the library door shouting for Rouster as he went. Ben was close behind and they waited in curious silence for the horsemen to approach.

*****

The stranger was one Oliver Cromwell, but beyond that, Marshall would say nothing until Roman could be found. He was mending fences along an isolated field.

"You want me to stop and come meet a stranger?"

A silent nod from the child who had been dispatched to fetch him.

"Are you hungry?" Roman had asked knowing the answer all ready. He indicated a nearby tree.

"There is a pouch of food and ale yonder. Bring it and tell me what you know."

And so they sat together discussing the lay of the land and eating the meal Rouster had assembled for Roman early that morning.

"You see, sire, 'tis strange." The boy put an entire plum in his mouth and it was a moment before he continued.

"They did not come by river, nor by the road. No, sire, they came through the Greenwich Wood, why, the King's own property." The lilt of the child's voice took on a suspicious tone.

"Um," Roman responded in kind. "Now why would they do that? Marshall has avoided coming that way for some time."

"Why, sire?"

Roman tousled the boy's hair.

"He believes there is trouble coming to the kingdom, lad." He stood and brushed the crumbs from his clothes.

"Now, see that you finish that meal there before you return to the manor."

It was early afternoon before Henrietta deemed Roman presentable for company. He had washed, trimmed his beard and put on a fresh set of clothing. His entrance into the library was welcomed by all – conversation had grown thin.

*****

"There is war now with Scotland?"

Cromwell fielded the question well even though he wondered if Baron de Grey lived under a rock, or perhaps on the moon. He had never met a more isolated or a stranger nobleman. His wife and children seemed to have as much authority as he, his servants were his friends, he introduced sheep into every conversation, and he seasoned his hatred of King Charles with neither tolerance nor caution.

"Yes, my lord, and there is talk of coming trouble for England as King Charles refuses to acknowledge the power of Parliament. He is of a hundred years ago."

Roman pinned his brilliant, glittering eyes on Cromwell.

"And what of Scotsmen living about here in the kingdom, eh? We heard a rumor that they, too, were being rounded up and forced to some false allegiance."

Cromwell nodded, wondering why such an issue would matter to an English Baron.

"Yes, there were several instances of that in London recently."

Roman rose and began pacing in front of the window.

"But . . ."

"Silence, please." It was the first time Cromwell had seen or heard the man exercise his natural rights as a member of the nobility. He continued to pace for some moments. No one spoke.

Finally, he returned to his seat. Agitation and anger were written clearly across his countenance. When he spoke, however, his voice was calm. Deadly calm, in fact.

"Oliver Cromwell, why are you here?"

The question was blunt and unexpected.

"Because, Baron, Marshall St. John speaks highly of you; because I believe the King must not be allowed to continue denigrating the rights of his people; because when war comes - and it will - I must know who will stand with the Parliamentarians, and who will support the rights of an errant king."

Roman looked at Marshall.

"And you?"

"I agree with Cromwell. And I believe 'tis important that he gauge accurately the mood of the country and the mood of the nobility. The time for consideration will have long since gone when these things come to crisis. If we are to win, we must know our friends. And our enemies."

Roman stood up, straightened his vest and set his jaw.

"Coudenoure is with you." He looked around the room at his family, his friends in turn. Henrietta rose and moved to his side with a slight nod. Behind her came Ben and Rouster, Ian and Elizabeth, Annabelle and Mary. All standing together, side by side.

Cromwell was deeply moved by the sight. Just when he had been ready to write them all off as a strange lot of artistic recluses and eccentric rustics, here they were standing united in determined support of their Baron and pledging faith with him. He had always considered Marshall St. John unlucky, for he had no woman and no family. But here was family. Here were friends. And here must be the core of what had made the man who he was. But Cromwell was also practical - and curious.

"From whence do you draw your hatred of King Charles? It seems unmitigated and intense."

"King Charles once took my land, threw my family out, brought about the death of my aunt and installed his whore at Coudenoure."

A furious cough erupted from the back of those gathered in the room. Annabelle. All turned.

"Pardon, pardon." She ran from the room. After a moment, Roman held forth his hand and Cromwell grasped it in both of his.

"We have much to discuss, Baron. 'Tis courageous of you to throw in with me so early. It will not be forgotten." Cromwell bowed in affirmation of his gratefulness.

"Yes, yes, but come. I will show you Coudenoure and you will sup with us before you leave."

He waved away Cromwell's objections.

"Besides, there is a new type of wool I have been working upon lately and Elizabeth tells me it takes the dye wonderfully . . ."

Elizabeth jumped in.

"Indeed, I will come with you, but let me get my notes on the subject so that I may explain my work with lanolin, which I believe is the key . . ."

"And I wish another opinion." Roman finished as though he had not been interrupted.

Despite the momentary return to normalcy, the life of Coudenoure was not destined to proceed along its wonted course, with Roman and his wool, Elizabeth with her workroom, Gabriella with her art. As they walked away, Ian moved to the window and wondered what was coming. Because he was from the north, would they come for him, too? Would Coudenoure suffer for his sake? He did not have to wait long for an answer.

*****

Cromwell returned to Greenwich alone that evening.

What a strange place, he thought. Strange . . . but wonderful. As he turned his horse at the foot of the drive he turned back to catch a final glimpse of Coudenoure. The sun was setting upon 'Quinn's' meadow, casting playful shadows to and fro. A shepherd boy could be seen in a far distant pasture bringing in his master's sheep. On the 'great ridge' on the estate's eastern side, children could be seen building a fire on its crest, dancing in the shadows that the sun began to send their way. Their distant shouts and cries echoed down the steep slope, past the building housing the newly-founded de Grey Publishers, and bounced their way to him. He smiled, remembering his own childhood play. The stately ruins of an aged chapel, skeletal in relief against the dying day, kept watch over the western edge of the estate. Odd how even in starkest form it yet sang hallelujah in an ethereal and silent language. A rising wind wrapped its sweet music round about it, intertwining its harmony with that of the mysterious and eternal music of the spheres. It was the language of the whole place, Cromwell decided: part of this world yet strangely apart from it. How would the coming wars affect it? Would its magic endure?

He turned away and made for Greenwich in the waning light.

Chapter Forty

The Next Morn

There was no warning.

In the rising dawn, the children were still abed in their parents' cottages behind the main house. The watch captain of their troop lay fast asleep beneath the covers of a narrow bed with his two brothers. In the next cottage, their captain slept peacefully with his stick sword beside him.

In the small room off the kitchen of the main house, Rouster had just begun to stir, kissing Mary before rising for the day. She smiled sleepily in return and snuggled deeper into the warmth of the bed. Henrietta, too, was just sliding from beside her mate and moving quietly to her perch at their window.

A loud banging upon the great wych elm front doors of the main house echoed loudly through the still and darkened rooms. Henrietta threw back the shutters and looked down on the front of the house to see what had caused the ruckus. Roman was beside her in a flash. Again the banging. Again.

Again. Roman pulled on his trousers and spoke quickly to Henrietta.

"Get the others up quickly. Get Marshall."

"Who are they? I cannot see them well."

"King's men. Now go." Roman flew from the room.

Marshall had heard the noise and was in the hallway before Roman.

"What do they want?" Roman said in terse tones as they raced down the stairs together.

At the door, Marshall handed him the candle and spoke in calm, commanding words.

"Open the door. Ask what they want. Tell them you must have a moment to gather yourself and close the door quickly."

"NO! I will . . ."

Marshall looked at him with eyes that would brook no dissent. Ben and Rouster were with them now and they knew the look well. As child warriors on the streets of London they had learned to trust and obey that very look, that very tone.

"Do it, Roman. Just do it." They spoke in unison. Annabelle appeared from nowhere and joined in their whispered chorus.

Roman opened the door as the others stepped into the black shadows of the hall and listened.

"Why do you beat upon my door thus?" Roman said sternly.

"Sir, are you Baron de Grey?"

"I am." They did not hear the quiet wariness in Roman's voice.

"England is under attack by Scotland."

"By a rabble of *bishops* I understand. *Quite* dangerous."

A sneer crossed the stranger's face.

"Indeed. Sire."

Roman was mentally noting their weapons, their number and size.

"We understand you may be giving quarter to the enemy. Is that true?"

"To a *bishop*?"

The man's frustration was growing.

No. Sire. A Scotsman. We understand he lives here on your estate. We have come to seize him for he may be a danger to England, as all Scotsmen might be at this moment."

"Yes, well, give me a moment to dress properly - I am still in my nightshirt, gentlemen - and I will assist you with your request."

You could almost see the relief and arrogant pleasure of victory cross the soldier's face.

"As you wish."

Roman closed the door.

"What do we have?" Marshall whispered.

"Eight men, three muskets and all have swords."

Marshall thought furiously.

"Where are the muskets I brought last Yuletide?"

What a stroke of luck that he had decided the children of the estate would enjoy such a show of modern arms at Christmas last. Ian spoke.

"They are in a storage bin in the stable. Both I and the stable master know how to shoot them."

Marshall was pure thought in action.

"Rouster, Ben, get the men in the cottages together now. Any weapon or tool will do. Tell them to hold up until they hear my signal."

"Annabelle . . ."

But she had already run well ahead of the ones just dispatched. Marshall turned to the children who had gathered. Their leader tied his yellow kerchief and stepped forward.

A loud banging on the door.

"Yes sir?"

"Get the babies and small children away to the woods. Send one of your best to Greenwich Palace, and tell him to speak to no one - NO ONE - except Oliver Cromwell. He is to relay these events to him."

The child nodded.

"Take the rest of your troop and set up position at the end of the cottage allee. Light torches and prepare to open the stables and barns and frighten the animals into the allee with them. Go - you have almost no time. But wait for my command before loosing the animals."

They were gone almost before he finished.

Another loud banging, this time accompanied by shouting.

"What shall I say?" asked Roman.

"Tell them the Scotsman will be delighted to meet them in the allee just behind the house."

As Marshall turned, he ran headlong into Annabelle with a stranger at her side, a woman. The two of them disappeared into the library and Marshall ran on through the kitchen and out the back door. As the banging began yet again, Roman opened the door.

The man on the stoop looked him up and down, as did his comrades.

"I see you did not change your clothing, sire."

"No."

The man hesitated before replying.

"So do you harbor a Scotsman?"

Silence. Surely the baron was not stupid enough to think he could take on men with muskets.

"Sire?"

"Yes. The man you seek lives behind this manor house in a small cottage."

With that, Roman closed the door, bolted it with a heavy medieval iron piece seldom if ever employed, and ran.

*****

The sun's rays had not topped the cottages' low roofs, leaving the allee in near darkness. A strange, preternatural stillness floated over the scene. The rogue troop of soldiers stepped to the point of entry into the allee and stood there, muskets loaded, swords drawn. From inside the barns and stables a rustling of animals could be heard as though a restless spirit had settled upon them. At the far end of the allee, a row of torches two deep burned in a brilliant line across the cobbled stones. In the dim light, it was not possible to discern who or what held them aloft.

Why were they there? Again, the baron surely would not take on armed men. He strained his eyes. Children! Children were holding those torches! He laughed. So the baron intended to fight with children and torches. He laughed again called out down the allee.

"Where are you? Do you mean to have these young ones fight for you? We have come to fetch you, you worthless Scotsman, and send you home."

"Home?" A man called forth in a defiant Scottish brogue. "*This* is my home."

"Aye, but we shall send you to a deep and eternal home." A snigger ran round the group. "Now come forward before you force my men to fire their weapons."

The hush of early morning was the only reply.

"You leave me no choice then. Forward, men!"

They were halfway down the allee before it occurred to any of them that the children, the torches, might have been set there as a diversion, a way to lure them into over-confidence and ensure they would enter the allee.

Marshall's plan was devious and brilliant. All he commanded did as they had been ordered. All he commanded stood ready for his signal. All he had commanded.

From a cottage doorway ran four figures: Henrietta, Elizabeth, Colleen and Gabriella. With swords and knives, they ran towards the soldiers screaming like banshees.

Then, it happened.

"'Tis a trap! Fire!"

"NOOOOO!!!!" Roman began running towards Henrietta.

The seconds slid slowly forward as the men turned their muskets on the approaching women.

"Fire I say!"

"Now! Now! Now!" Marshall yelled.

But even as the words floated on the moment, two other female figures sliced through the world that lay between life and death, between the muskets and the approaching line. From their uncovered flank, in one swift and furious move, Alexandra threw her entire weight behind the heavy long sword she had collected moments earlier from above the library mantel. She brought it down with a decisive clang upon the muskets even as she threw herself against the man nearest her. Like dominoes, they fell as their shots rang out. And as they rang out, the second figure hurled itself upon the last musket in the row, taking a direct blow from its blast. Annabelle.

Chaos descended. Sheep, horses, men, torches, muskets - all came at the disordered troop from every side. They were trampled beneath a storm of fury and hooves.

For good or ill, the die had been cast irrevocably cast. But from this time hence, the healing of Ian's heart had finally begun, being knit back together even against its own will by the depth of the love and the willingness to sacrifice themselves for him on the part of all who, along with Ian, called Coudenoure their home.

Chapter Forty-One

January 30, 1649

Tuesday

Damp and cold, the day drew on. Charles sat on the deep sill of his bedchamber window drinking tea. For a moment, he leaned his head against the icy glass and closed his eyes, wondering what had brought him to this moment. And it had all begun so well! He drifted in time.

Before him danced an image of his first love, Alexandra of Malta. Ummm. Yes. Alexandra, dark, voluptuous, promising all with that dark mien of some faraway place. He could still smell her skin, her scent of rare and exotic flowers. He preferred not to think of her as he last saw her. Where was she now, he wondered? Had she gone to the party before him? He giggled at the irreverent thought.

Why could she not just have been happy with that estate he had stolen for her – stolen clean away from some baron! He smiled at the audacious nature of what he had done in his youth. But of course, he had had George. He could not have done it without George.

Even now, twenty years on, Charles could not stand the pain of his friend's assassination - had it happened yesterday it could not be more immediate, more horrifying. Still he was disconsolate and he wondered if he would be here now, imprisoned in St. James Palace, had George stayed with him. He doubted it very much.

What would happen to the monarchy when he was gone? Strangely, he cared less about that than he did about his 'things' - those bits and pieces of art, the odd palace here and there, the tapestries, the clothing, that he had accumulated over his lifetime.

In that respect, He had done well indeed and was proud yet of his rapacious hunger for masterpieces and its resulting collection. Pieces from across the continent - Titian, Rubens, Raphael. And of course, the Van Dyck's and Le Sueur's . . . what would happen to them all? He remembered laughing with George at the discomfort the Duke of Mantua must have felt, the anguish no doubt, of having to break up and part with his magnificent collection, almost all of which Charles had purchased. He now understood what before he could only ridicule in ignorance. Yes. So long ago.

Why? He opened his eyes and sipped the tea that now had grown cold. Why?

His father had been a nightmare of a king. He was a drunkard, a brawler, an ineffectual monarch on his best days. The man had cared only for the hunt, and on his dying day was still awed by the sheer ostentatious wealth of England. England, with its country estates, its refined manners and incredible palaces. But James, his father, had *survived.* He had managed Parliament and threaded his way carefully and successfully through the religious conflicts of his day. The crown treasury was as empty as a drum at his death, but the monarchy was intact. So why had this happened to him, James?

His father had been an absolutist as he himself was. Why, the divine right of kings was evident in the very fabric of society - what would the world be if God's vessels did not set the law and rule above all others? Such a society could not survive. Could it?

He almost hissed as he thought of the new world across the vast ocean. It was a world unfolding to a rhythm no one had ever heard before. They travelled there for freedom - *religious* freedom! It was an abomination before God that a place had been found where he, James, could not with ease reach out and smite them for their heresy. But it was not just religious freedom which the winds whispered of these days, but a broader, more confounding one. It was this, yes, this foul spirit of rebellion, that had brought him low.

Parliament believed they had rights, that the people had rights. What ridiculous folderol! He had been right to rule on his own without them. And then, when he did allow them to enter into session, the ungrateful fools had insisted on being heard, had actually given him a writ with their demands. Apostasy! Heresy!

He shook his head and poured himself another cup. If his father had not left the coffers empty, his heir would not have been at the mercy of that body of scoundrels. If, if, if.

It was all over now. Done. They would come for him soon, the guards, and escort him to Whitehall where they would perform regicide. Oh, God, let them suffer at your hands! Let the bastards feel your wrath at taking the life of their sovereign! He closed the door tightly against thoughts of that moment, for there was time enough to consider it when his head was on the block. Time enough indeed.

*****

The guards did appear, that afternoon, to escort King Charles to Whitehall. As he looked out over the sea of faces come to watch his gruesome execution, he closed his life with the words that had echoed down the years of his reign, the words that most fundamentally tore the crown asunder and caused his own death:

"A subject and a sovereign are clean different things."

Epilogue

Spring 1650

The lavender was early this year, as was the entire meadow, for winter had been unseasonably mild. The daffodils were gone and in their place came the fritillaries, the larkspur, the wild hyssop and the liatris. A million unknown meadow flowers accompanied them, some tiny, some quite large, but all contributing to the symphonic beauty that was Quinn's meadow in full bloom. The day was spring cool, with a clean breeze that smelled of thyme and rosemary, strawberries, flowers. The sun shone forth in a cloudless sky.

On the gravel sweep which fronted the manor house a small metal table sat around which three chairs were gathered.

"I tell you, the score is quite clear, Rouster. See here, I have kept the tally as always." Ben held a grubby paper and pencil out to Rouster for inspection. Marshall pushed his chair back, stretched his legs and looked on in amusement. He turned his face skyward while he waited, soaking up the warmth from the sun. Checking the score of their card game was a ritual which played itself out each day at the same time in the same place. The three urchins, Marshall laughed to himself. Urchins indeed.

With the civil wars had come an end to his position at Greenwich Palace as stable master. It was natural, when Coudenoure lost hers, that Marshall step in. Rouster no longer ran the day-to-day affairs of the kitchen but supervised from afar as his son grew into the father before him. And Ben, as always and forever, was lost amongst the books and manuscripts of Coudenoure. Each afternoon, they gathered for gossip and cards on the graveled way. Rouster was calling his name.

"Marshall, pay attention man! We are back at play!"

Some moments passed in intense card play. Ben eventually interrupted.

"This reminds me of the day we met at my place beneath the bridge in London. We were playing for the last cup of broth, do you remember? And that gang of ruffians came along."

"No, no," Rouster assured him, "I remember the day well. Aye it was something. But we played not for broth but for biscuit. And they were not ruffians, they were . . ."

Ben interrupted him.

"Marshall, do you remember? And you commanded them to . . ."

"No," Marshall was certain, "I simply said . . ."

The front doors opened and little Roman ran lightly to his father with a book under his arm.

"Papa, where is Ian? I must discuss this passage with him! He told me it was dactylic hexameter but I believe it reads better *my* way."

Ben tousled his son's dark and wavy hair while kissing him on the cheek.

"He is at the publishing shop, Roman."

Without waiting for more, the child skipped on. Ben gazed after him with pride. Rouster looked at his friend and smiled.

"A late blessing indeed." He said. Ben nodded.

Up the drive came a clatter of hooves from an open carriage.

"And what does the good friar want today, do you suppose, um?" asked Marshall. "If he is here to convert me, I fear he is too late."

The rig stopped immediately before them. Friar Dunston stepped from one side, while an older, yet handsome woman exited from the other.

"Do wait, Deborah. 'Tis not seemly for a woman to simply help herself from a carriage."

The woman in question ignored him and with reluctance, he presented her to the urchins.

"My sister, sirs, Deborah."

They rose and bowed. Deborah tucked an errant strand of chestnut hair behind her ear and took in the table before her.

"You know, if you play the Diamond, I believe you will have the suite."

All three men looked at their cards laughing.

"So you know the game?" Marshall asked pleasantly, standing again and pulling the fourth chair out for her with an enquiring smile. She smiled back and he noticed how it lit up her face. She had lovely green eyes, and an upturned nose. It was impossible to see the wrinkles through her bright countenance. As she nodded and made to sit down, Friar Dunston spoke.

"No, no, no. I mean, Deborah, there are women about on the estate. Wouldn't you like to meet them? 'Tis not seemly . . ."

Marshall thought he heard a quiet, defiant, 'Pish,' escape the woman's lips.

Without waiting and without reason, he spoke.

"Madame . . ."

"Mademoiselle," she said and blushed. "An old maid, I am afraid." But she was cheerful as she spoke, as though she could not be happier or more content with her status.

"Ah, and I am an old bachelor, so we shall get on splendidly! I will be happy to be your guide, show you the estate, and introduce round about. We are having a spring festival on the ridge this evening – quite heathen but perhaps you and your brother . . ."

"Heathen?" the friar frowned.

"Oh, if it be heathen, then by all means." Deborah said gaily. Marshall laughed at the audacity of the woman while her brother spoke broadly to the group.

"I have tried in vain to change her views, but she goes her own way. I am not certain if she gives a fig for religion."

Deborah jumped in.

"I do indeed, dear brother, just not yours."

Marshall bowed and the two of them stepped away towards the manor house.

"So the good friar is your brother?"

"Oh yes. I have tried in vain to change his views, but he goes his own way."

Inexplicably, wonderfully, they fell into conversation as though they had always known one another, would always know one another, were meant to be.

Henrietta, Elizabeth and Mary sat before the fire in Elizabeth's workshop, discussing children, the estate, weaving, art, wherever their thoughts took them. Mary darned a sock of Rouster's while Elizabeth fussed with a knot of yarn. Henrietta rocked contentedly and pulled her shawl about her.

"So Colleen will marry, um?" Mary asked.

"Finally!" Elizabeth's response was met with merriment.

"The war interrupted everything." Henrietta observed. "Nevertheless, all things in good time."

"And Gabriella? Is there a man who can tame such a spirit?" Elizabeth asked.

"Aye, but he will be special. He must needs be so."

"Well, where is he?" Elizabeth asked pointedly. "If he is coming he should make haste, for none of us grows younger."

"He will come, he will come," Henrietta reached out and patted her daughter's hand.

"And Annabelle?" Mary asked. "I am afraid my daughter cares not a fig for marriage."

Elizabeth nodded.

"I believe you are right, my friend. However, she is happy. And we are surely blessed that she survived the musket blast."

"We are doubly blessed," Henrietta interjected, "For her, and for Alexandra. God's knees! I never thought I would say such a thing but 'tis true! If not for them, I would be dead these past years. Dead and gone, never having seen little Roman, never having learned to forgive. Never learning to move on."

They sat in silence.

"Where are they now? In the cottage?" Mary asked.

"I believe so. Annabelle passed through here earlier today and we discussed the various colors of rouge they have been concocting. They are quite talented, the two of them. 'Tis a pity that more women do not wear such makeup, for they have perfected a number of condiments: lash darkener, rouge, a powder to smooth fine lines. And they give it all a lovely lavender scent."

"They could sell it, you know. I believe they could turn a profit."

"Is Alexandra still . . . ?" Elizabeth circled her finger about her ear.

"A bit, but then she has had a hard life. If she lives sometimes in the past, who are we to decree otherwise?"

Henrietta's thoughts encircled her family's estate, performing a mental inventory of those she loved.

"And Roman? Where is my good husband?"

"Ah, he is on the ridge, Henrietta, supervising the bonfire and the arrangements for tonight's festival."

The party would be a propitious opportunity.

"We shall announce Colleen's engagement, then, and set the bans shortly."

"What is his name again?" asked Mary.

"Ethan. He was an accountant for the royal house and Marshall knows him well. He predicts that they will be quite happy together and says that Ethan is a good man."

*****

As dusk came upon them, all gathered on the great ridge. The fire burned brightly; the children played; the mighty Thames flowed sluggishly past. The great cathedral ruins rose against the evening sky, ethereal and beautiful. A shepherd herded a small flock in for the night. Far below, they watched Ian come from the cemetery. He waved up at them and they knew he would join them anon. On the gravel drive strolled a lone figure in a full hoop skirt with a tattered parasol. They listened quietly, respectfully, as the sound of Alexandra calling for her golden carriage floated upwards on the evening air.

Much later, as the fire roared and the stars twinkled, promising a bright future, a kitchen boy filled their glasses. Roman raised his.

"To Coudenoure!"

All glasses raised, all hearts gave thanks.

"To Coudenoure!"

#####

[To be continued by Royal Sagas 5: "Restoration", coming in Spring 2018. And look for the Royal Sagas prequel, "Thomas de Grey of Bosworth Field", coming in Fall 2017]

CPSIA information can be obtained
at www.ICGtesting.com
Printed in the USA
LVHW052147290519
619528LV00029B/713/P

9 781548 476854